N47704

D1138594

47704

The
Dragon Tattoo

Look out for more Baker Street Mysteries

Coming soon . . .

The Rose of Africa
The Shape of Evil

THE BAKER STREET MYSTERIES

The
Dragon Tattoo

Tim Pigott-Smith

Illustrated by Chris Mould

Hodder
Children's
Books

A division of Hachette Children's Books

Copyright © 2008 Tim Pigott-Smith
Illustrations copyright © 2008 Chris Mould

First published in Great Britain in 2008
by Hodder Children's Books

The right of Tim Pigott-Smith and Chris Mould to be identified as the Author
and Illustrator of the Work has been asserted by them in accordance with the
Copyright, Designs and Patents Act 1988

Sherlock Holmes, Doctor Watson, Mrs Hudson are trademarks of the
Sir Arthur Conan Doyle Literary Estate and are used under licence from
The Administrators of the Sir Arthur Conan Doyle Copyrights,
c/o Jonathan Clowes Ltd, London.

I

All rights reserved. Apart from any use permitted under UK copyright
law, this publication may only be reproduced, stored or transmitted, in
any form, or by any means with prior permission in writing from the
publishers or in the case of reprographic production in accordance with
the terms of licences issued by the Copyright Licensing Agency and may
not be otherwise circulated in any form of binding or cover other than
that in which it is published and without a similar condition being
imposed on the subsequent purchaser.

All characters in this publication are fictitious and any resemblance
to real persons, living or dead, is purely coincidental.

A Catalogue record for this book is available from the British Library

ISBN-13: 978 0 340 95703 5

Typeset in Garamond by Avon DataSet Ltd,
Bidford on Avon, Warwickshire

Printed in the UK by CPI Bookmarque, Croydon, CR0 4TD

The paper and board used in this paperback by Hodder Children's Books
are natural recyclable products made from wood grown in
sustainable forests. The manufacturing processes conform to the
environmental regulations of the country of origin.

Hodder Children's Books
a division of Hachette Children's Books
338 Euston Road, London NW1 3BH
An Hachette Livre UK Company

To My Family.
And Arthur Conan Doyle, without whom . . .

PROLOGUE

LONDON – 1891
THE ISLE OF DOGS

D usk. Dank and misty. Street urchin, Sam Wiggins, runs for his life – the small bag of stolen chestnuts still warm in his hand . . .

Sam has shaken off all but one of his pursuers. With a rapid glance over his shoulder – almost losing his footing – he nips between two buildings, into a narrow gap that he hopes the man behind him does not know about. But when he emerges at the other end, and pauses to catch his breath, he can still hear the flat thump of heavy leather boots coming down the passage behind him. He sets off again, shooting in through the doorway of a slaughterhouse.

He darts between hanging carcasses of meat, his worn shoes slipping on the blood-soaked floor. A beam of light catches the blade of a huge cleaver, splits the gloom and temporarily blinds him. A man, armed with a giant meat-saw, blocks his path, but he dodges round him and plunges outside, into the lane that runs between the backs of all the warehouses. Now, at last, he can hear nothing behind him, but still, he dares not stop running.

Ahead of him Sam suddenly sees a large figure. His pursuer has anticipated his short cut through the slaughterhouse and now stands barring his way. Sam screeches to a standstill and sets off in the opposite direction as fast as he can, with his adversary close behind, closer now than ever. He has got to know these streets well, but this sudden change of direction disorientates him and he takes a wrong turn. To his horror, he finds himself in a dead-end. The unrelenting boots echo behind him. Shoving the bag of chestnuts into his jacket pocket, Sam runs, leaps and grabs the top of the alley wall. He loses precious seconds trying to haul himself up. He can think of nothing but his pursuer, whose enormous hand now grabs his calf, and he is not aware that the stolen chestnuts are spilling out below him. Sam just manages to shake free, kicking and scrabbling over the wall, dropping down into a builder's yard. Landing on a mountain of sand, he finds it hard to move fast. His feet glue down in the shifting sand, but he ploughs on, ducking and diving between piles of cement sacks and a stack of bricks that wobble precariously as he swings round them. He tears out of the yard, as the night-watchman emerges from his hut, brandishing a stick and cursing.

Sam knows that just ahead there is a long, narrow alley. He reaches the corner and plunges down it. The sound of his feet echoes louder and louder and the downward slope gives him an extra turn of speed. He reaches the bottom flat out and, half looking back over his shoulder, he rounds the corner, running headlong into a tall, thin gentleman, wearing a large cape and a deerstalker hat. Although Sam thunders into him at full pelt, the man does not budge an inch; it is Sam – who is much smaller, and thin from lack of food – who is thrown off balance and sent sprawling in to the gutter.

'Foolish boy,' says the gentleman, contemptuously. As Sam scrabbles to his feet, the man seizes him by the collar. 'Stop wriggling, boy!'

'Let go of me!' cries Sam. 'There's someone after me.'

'Nonsense.' Holding Sam by the scruff of the neck, the gentleman drags him, struggling, back to the corner at the bottom of the alley. 'Look,' he says sharply. Reluctantly, Sam looks. There is nothing. No one. He cannot believe it. His pursuer has disappeared. He relaxes a little, and as a consequence, so does the gentleman's iron grip. His tone, however, is still condescending. 'A quite unnecessary panic, I suspect.'

Staring up the deserted alley, Sam protests, 'He was there.'

'A figment of your imagination.'

'He was there!' Beginning to get his breath back, Sam looks at the stranger properly for the first time. His face is white, his eyes piercing, and his long, pointed nose, haughty. He looks down it at Sam and speaks coolly.

'If you had, for one moment, resisted your childish fear and paused in your flight to listen, you would have heard, as I did, only one set of footsteps – your own.'

Sam is proud, and he doesn't like being talked down to in this way. He is on the point of answering back, when a much shorter, stockier man, whom he has not noticed before, catches his eye. This man, who sports a well-clipped moustache, is warm and friendly.

'I think you're being rather hard on the boy, Holmes. I could hear at least two lots of feet. Maybe more.'

'The echo, Watson,' says the gentleman in the deerstalker dismissively, 'the echo.'

'What?'

'There was no one but the boy himself. *His* imagination and *your* ears are equally at fault, Watson.

He was frightened by the sound of his own feet.'

'The echo! Of course,' replies Watson. 'How foolish of me.'

'I wasn't making it up,' Sam insists.

'If you were not making it up, then where is your pursuer?' enquires the white-faced gentleman with disdain. Sam is choked. He knows only too well that he was being chased. He knows why, but his pursuer is nowhere to be seen. He can't speak. Because he is unable to reply, the gentleman mutters under his breath, 'The boy is safe, and we have business to attend to,' and moves briskly away. 'Come along, Watson.'

'I wasn't making it up, Mr Watson,' pleads Sam.

'I believe you,' says Watson kindly. 'But unfortunately, you have no *evidence*.'

'Watson! We have not a moment to lose.'

'Coming, Holmes,' says Watson cheerily. Then to Sam, 'Will you be all right now?'

'I *have* got evidence though, sir,' says Sam, putting his hand in his pocket for the little bag of chestnuts. But his pocket is empty. The chestnuts are not there. Watson is looking expectantly at the lad, but it will take too long for Sam to explain. 'Nothing, sir,' he says quietly, 'it don't matter.'

Sam falls sullen and silent. His pride is dented again.

He is cross with himself because it looks as though he is lying. He feels sick with shame, and loses his balance for a moment. He sways suddenly as if he is going to pass out.

Watson puts his hand out to steady the boy. 'When did you last eat?' he asks.

'Nearly two days ago. I stole some food,' Sam confesses. 'That's why I was running away. But I've dropped it.' Sam is certain that Watson will be cross with him, and he stands, feeling dizzy, weak and stupid, waiting for even more humiliation. To his surprise, Watson is sympathetic.

'Poor boy, poor boy. Here. Take this.' From the pocket of his waistcoat, Watson produces two pennies, which he places in Sam's hand. 'It's not a lot, but it will buy you something to eat, and you won't have to steal. Spend this one, and if at all possible, save the other, as my dear mother used to say.'

'Watson! I am waiting,' calls the gentleman in the deerstalker.

'Coming, Holmes. I am sorry, boy. I must go.'

'It's not your fault, sir,' says Sam. 'You've been really decent. Thank you, Mr Watson.'

Sam watches as Watson moves away. His benefactor, who has a distinctly military air about him, turns back, smiling, and says, 'By the way, it's not Mister.'

'Sorry?'

'I am not Mister Watson, I am *Doctor* Watson. Goodbye.'

'Goodbye, sir. And thank you.'

It was not until some hours later, when he had finally eaten something, that Sam pieced it together. When he had decided to try and live in dockland, there had been talk of a series of gruesome murders – indeed people talked of little else. The villain – a serial murderer whose grisly exploits with a meat-axe had terrorized the dockland community for nearly a year – had just been apprehended, but fear still gripped that whole sweep of the river known as the Isle of Dogs. The crime had finally been solved by the famous detective, Sherlock Holmes. Holmes was notorious for wearing an Aberdeen cape and a deerstalker hat. Watson – *Doctor* Watson – had addressed the haughty man with the pale face and the long, thin nose as Holmes, and this man had been wearing a cape and deerstalker. Sam was obliged to conclude that the person he had barged into – the man with the disdainful air and iron grip – was *Sherlock* Holmes, the celebrated consulting detective. In which case, the nice man, Dr Watson, had to be the well-known writer, who recorded all Holmes's adventures. How Sam wished he could read them, but of course, he had no skill with letters, although he was determined to learn.

Sam's life was difficult. Every minute of it was a struggle. He found it hard to believe that, even for a moment, he had so much as spoken with two people from the other side of the tracks, two wealthy people, two well-known people. It was even harder to believe that one of them had been so nice to him; the whole incident seemed like some figment of his imagination – the theft, the chase, the encounter in the half-light of dusk. However, unlike the futile theft of chestnuts, unlike the nightmare chase, Sam had evidence of the encounter – two pennies. *They* were real enough.

Sam followed Watson's advice to the letter. With one of the pennies he bought food, and with the other, he began to save. He was determined that somehow he would make his way out of the poverty and homelessness that he so hated, and in which he felt trapped. And he dreamed. He dreamed about becoming a doctor, like his benefactor Dr Watson. And he saved, to try and make the dream come true.

TWO YEARS LATER ...

1

THE HOWLING DOG

greeny-yellow fog swirled up from the River Thames. It clung to the walls, it smeared the paving stones, it crept under doors. A 'pea-souper' was what the rivermen called these foul-smelling vapours. They were enough to keep all but the desperate or determined in their homes: thirteen-year-old Sam Wiggins was a bit of both. When he'd run away from home, Sam had deliberately chosen a remote corner of London in which to hide – Limehouse, near the docks. He could easily lose himself there, so he stayed, even though he didn't like it. It was as though something terrible had happened there – a plague, or a murder. He heard a rumour that over three hundred years before, old King Henry, in his palace down at Hampton, was disturbed by the barking of his dogs. To get a good night's sleep, he moved them to kennels on the other side of London. Which was how the spot where Sam had his hideout got its name – the Isle of Dogs. After two years, he was settled – stuck, you might say.

The East End of Victorian London was a lethal place. If you were homeless, it was hell. Sam was always tempted to steal just to survive. He still took dreadful risks occasionally, just to eat, and in order to protect his puny savings. He had managed to teach himself to read, he dreamed of being a doctor, and he was desperate not to get on the wrong side of the law. The places where they sent kids who were caught pilfering were even more terrifying than being homeless. Sam knew the horrors first-hand. He'd been living in the parish workhouse with his mum when she took the beadle, who ran it, for her second husband. Sam had adored his real dad, so when his new dad – the beadle – took his belt to Sam's back, he decided it was time to leave. He was frightened out on the street, but he felt more his own master. He'd been starving, he'd been ill, he'd even been beaten up, but he'd survived. He had learned who and what his enemies were, although there was one enemy over which he had no control – the weather. And it didn't get worse than this fog.

Only someone who knew the streets blindfolded would have risked going out at all in such filthy weather with darkness approaching, but Sam had business. He was slowly making his way towards the docks, feeling for a narrow passage that ran between two warehouses. He couldn't see it, he just knew it was there. He found it, slipped into it, and moved cautiously forward, sliding his hand along the mouldy wall to help him keep his bearings. Sam knew every stinking alley and vile corner of the Isle of Dogs. He had also got to know the locals – the boatmen, the carters, the ladies of the street, the law. And he'd survived by making sure *they* knew *him*, by doing them the odd favour, by making himself indispensable. He knew the rogues too, the local gangs. He knew where they hung out, the pubs, the gambling rooms, the opium dens. As he edged his way out of the passage and on to the greasy cobblestones of Black Lane, he could hear a dog howling, not far away. A dog? It was ghostly, almost human: long cries of pain that made his flesh creep. 'Blasted fog,' he said to himself. 'It plays tricks on you.'

Sam was a loner. Always had been. He was tall for his age, thin, pallid, with sharp features and dark hair swept back from his forehead, tied off in a ponytail.

Tonight, with a ragged strip of cotton round his nose and mouth to protect his lungs, he looked like a right villain, but the fog was so dense, no one could see him. The acrid reek of chlorine cut through his meagre protection and caught the back of his throat. He turned up the collar of his battered tweed jacket and moved on down towards the river, where the fog was likely to be even thicker. Sam's destination was an old Thames wherry – a big, light barge with a sail – moored in a nearby wharf. The captain of the wherry had a job for him. Dockland was deserted. No one else would have bothered to keep an appointment on an evening like this, but letting people down wasn't Sam's style. The Captain wanted Sam's help. Sam had told him he would be there, and not even this fog was going to stop him.

On the wealthier, west side of London, it was almost as bad. Fog has no respect for money, as Billy Chizzell, the page-boy at 221b Baker Street, discovered when he popped out to buy a newspaper for his employer. He could hear the street vendor's cry – 'Evenin' papers! Get your evenin' papers!' – but couldn't *see* the paper seller from ten yards away. Back at 221b, as he trudged upstairs to the study, Billy noticed the headlines, which suggested that burning less coal might reduce the smog. He shrugged. Most people's fireplaces, like the furnaces and factory chimneys, were still belching smoke.

One man, however, was prepared to endure the cold for the sake of his fellow men, and this was the gentleman to whom Billy handed the paper – John Watson. As a doctor in general practice, Watson had seen the effects of these fogs on his patients; he had watched too many of the children die, coughing blood.

This evening, quiet and preoccupied, Watson barely noticed Billy's arrival, which was unlike him. Billy was pretty sure he knew why Watson was behaving so out of character. More than a week ago, Billy's other employer, Sherlock Holmes, with whom Dr Watson shared rooms, had gone out late one afternoon and had not returned. Holmes was Billy's hero, the man that more than any other in the world he wanted to be like. Holmes's ability to solve mysteries, using nothing more than his powers of observation and deduction, brought pleas for his help from all over the world. It was common for Holmes to be called away suddenly, but it was uncommon for him to leave no explanation.

His early-evening surgery over, the troubled doctor

sat wrapped in a heavy tartan rug. And that was how he remained after Billy delivered the paper – staring at the unlit fire, the newspaper unopened on his knee. Watson was indeed thinking about his missing friend – Sherlock Holmes. He could draw only two conclusions from Holmes's long silence: either the detective was *unable* to communicate with him or he *did not wish* to. Both possibilities were distressing.

Through the tall windows that usually looked out on to the bustle of Baker Street, Watson watched the clouds of sulphurous fog turning black with the December night. Unsettled, he rose and rang the bell to summon the housekeeper, Mrs Hudson. Moments later, as he was drawing the heavy velvet curtains to shut out the loathsome mists and vapours, he heard her sharp knock at the door.

'Come in, Mrs Hudson!' he called. The door was opened by a short, plumpish woman, impeccably uniformed in her apron and starched white cap. Behind her, on the landing, Watson caught a glimpse of Billy Chizzell, equally smart in his green page-boy uniform with its rows of silver buttons and pill-box hat. As Mrs Hudson entered the room, Watson added in a whisper, 'And, Mrs H, please shut the door. I do not wish Billy to hear.' Mrs Hudson did as she was asked.

'Mrs Hudson, I am most deeply concerned about Mr Holmes. Nine days, and still no word.'

The door may have been firmly closed, but Billy's ears were equally firmly glued to the keyhole. He heard all the fears for Holmes's safety that Dr Watson confided to Mrs Hudson, and decided that if his master and hero was missing, he, Billy Chizzell, was going to do something about it.

Even in the candlelit glow of the Captain's cabin, Sam fancied he could still hear a dog howling. If the Captain could hear it, he didn't appear to. He heated a fishy broth on his little galley stove, placed a brimming bowl on the table in front of Sam, sat down opposite, and watched him eat. The Captain had a ruddy, carbuncled face. When he spoke, it was with a rich West Country drawl.

'If ye turn up early next Friday, moi lad, then this silver sixpence . . .' he placed a coin on the table between them, 'is yours. Take good 'n' proper care o' moi little boat, and when oi gets back from settling moi affairs, then this . . .' and he placed another gleaming sixpence in front of Sam, 'will go with it.'

Sam couldn't take his eyes off the money. He could live off one sixpence for a week, and put the other in the sock where he hid his savings. He sipped at the thick soup – the first warm food he had tasted that day. Apart from the Captain's patient breathing, and the occasional creak of the wherry, there was no other sound in the cabin until Sam's spoon scraped the bottom of the steel bowl.

'Well?' said the Captain.

'Friday, sir,' replied Sam. 'I'll be here. What you got on board?'

'Cargo of sugar for 'ee to take care of.'

Sam himself had been tempted to steal sugar from barges: when the tide was out, and the boats lay grounded on the river-bed, you just jumped on board, cut holes in the sugar sacks and scooped the sugar into every pocket, hat or bag you could carry. Lots of kids that Sam knew, who were hard up, used to practise this simple theft, and the right dealer would pay a halfpenny a pound.

'Sugar. Right,' said Sam and rose, ready to go. 'And thanks for the grub.'

Fog was seeping ominously round the edges of the cabin door. It seemed to get everywhere, even inside, contaminating everything with a thin grey film.

'Would ye like to bed down 'ere tonight?' asked the Captain. 'Ye can have the other bunk.'

Sam shook his head. 'No thanks, sir. I got to be somewhere else.' The Captain knew he was lying, and admired his pride. 'Bye, sir,' said Sam. 'And thanks again.'

'Ye be a good lad, Sam Wiggins. Older than your years.'

'I'll see you Friday, sir,' said Sam.

As the Captain opened the cabin door, the night was pierced by another chilling howl, more human than ever. Neither spoke, but they both sensed that some crime was being committed, some act of evil, hidden from the eyes of the world by this repellent fog. Sam hesitated.

'Just a dog,' he said.

The Captain didn't look convinced. 'It's a bad noight to be abroad, young Sam. Do ye know what they say about a dog, howling in the noight?'

'No, sir.'

'Well, they do say it means a death.' Sam looked very pale. 'Ye want to change your moind and stay?'

'No thank you, sir. I'll be all right, sir,' said Sam, edging nervously outside.

'Go careful then, lad.' The Captain closed the door and returned to his cosy cabin. Sam covered his mouth, hunched his shoulders and set off bravely down the gangplank. He feared another howl would split the night, but instead there was a brooding silence, which was just as eery.

Sam set off slowly through the fogbound wastes of dockland. During the two dark and lonely years since he first came here, Sam had been befriended by Ann-li, a young Chinese girl. The Chinese were often disliked and distrusted, just because they were Chinese, and Ann-li was, in her way, as much of an outsider as Sam. One night, Sam had rescued her from some hooligans. Mr and Mrs Chang – Ann-li's mum and dad – were thankful; they fed Sam, and took care of him. There weren't many people in this part of the world who were charitable to strangers, and Sam felt real gratitude to the close-knit Chang family.

Sam was heading back to his hideout. He edged his way along the waterfront and turned by the water pump, up into Skittle Alley. As Chang's Seamen's Hostel was on his way, Sam intended to drop in. The last time he'd seen Ann-li, she had said she needed to talk to him, and Sam had the impression that it was about something pretty troubling. But then he'd had a job out of London, breaking coal for a coalmonger, and he'd not had time to catch up with his friend.

It was Ann-li's uncle Fu who let him in. Sam knew

immediately that something was wrong. Uncle Fu – everyone called him Uncle Fu – was normally friendly and welcoming, but this evening, as he ushered Sam past the pipe smokers in the crowded, gloomy front room, he was quiet and withdrawn. Sam had grown used to the strangeness of this place. He knew that these dreamy-looking people, puffing at their hookahs, had no idea he was there, no notion that the building in which they lay, cocooned in sweet-smelling warmth, was besieged by fog. They were beyond caring. Fu, in padded slippers, small square black cap and pigtail, glided between them, his silken robes brushing them softly as he led Sam to the stairs. He ushered him up without a word, and turned back to tend the pipes.

Upstairs, Mrs Chang was feeding Ann-li's baby brother. She acknowledged Sam but, unusually, didn't smile. In answer to Sam's question, she merely pointed upwards. Sam found Ann-li in her tiny attic room.

'Sam! You shouldn't be here.'

'Why not? What's wrong?'

'Some men are with my father.'

'Who?'

'I don't know.'

'Who are they, Ann-li? What's wrong?'

'They won't tell me,' said Ann-li, then added sadly,

'but soon, I guess, we shall be moving on.'

'What d'you mean?'

'Always we settle. Make home. For a while things go well. Then men come for my father. I don't understand. They don't tell.'

'Who are these men?' Ann-li looked as if she wanted to answer but couldn't. 'Who are they, Ann-li?' Still Ann-li did not respond. Sam realised it was because she was listening. '*Where* are they?'

Ann-li sat motionless for a moment, then said, 'Come. I show. But no sound. Or we make worse. These men I hate. One of them – a big man – is just big and stupid, I think. His name is Dooley. The other – I can't think of him without feeling scared – he is so creepy. And he is *not* stupid.'

'Do you know his name?'

'He is a colonel. He was in the army, I guess, and he calls himself Colonel still, although he is now working for very different people.'

'What?' said Sam, mystified. 'Who?'

'A Chinese gang. They call themselves the Dragons. But I am just guessing. I don't really know. They not tell me. This is what I overhear.'

'Do you know his name?'

'Maltravers. Colonel Maltravers. You still want

to go see?' Ann-li clearly did *not* want to go and see at all. Sam was a bit frightened, but he was curious. He nodded.

They crept down the narrow ladder from Ann-li's attic and then out through a window, on to the flat roof of the soot-blackened outbuildings at the rear. Ann-li paused. She held her fingers to her lips and pointed. The swirling fog was lit up by the dull yellow glow coming through a dirt-engrained skylight. Too frightened to look herself, Ann-li ushered Sam forward. Creeping closer, Sam looked down through the cloudy glass.

In the small room below, Sam could see two men with Ann-li's father, Chang, who was white with fear. Towering over him was the biggest man Sam had ever seen. From this giant's right ear, a jagged scar ran across his face, into the corner of his mouth. The knife which had slashed his cheek in a gang brawl had taken the tip of his tongue off. Dooley had never been handsome or talkative; now he was disfigured, and at this moment silent. It was the other man – Colonel Edmund Maltravers – who was doing the talking. Sam laid his ear close to the corner of the window, trying to hear what was being said. Maltravers – a bald, mean-faced man, with lidless eyes –

hissed at Ann-li's father. 'Do as I ask, Chang.'

Sam could only just hear Chang's mumbled reply. 'I a-am sorry, Colonel. I cannot.'

Sam looked back at Ann-li and beckoned her forward. Ann-li shook her head. Suddenly, Maltravers's voice rose loud, spitting with fury. 'Answer me, Chang, you little fool. Are you not aware of how small a thing you are being asked to do?' Sam was hypnotized by the sheer sense of evil emanating from the man.

'It is not how small a thing, Colonel, but how bad,' Chang replied. 'I will not take children from their parents, from those who love them. Other things I have done for you, bad things, but this I cannot do.'

Sam's mind reeled. What did Maltravers mean? Take children away from their parents? Chang was a kind man. What bad things had he *already* done? Afraid, Sam watched as Maltravers turned his back on Chang and picked up a pair of hand bellows that he applied to the small fire that was smouldering in the grate. Nothing was said as Maltravers heated the embers. What was he going to do? For one moment Sam suspected that Maltravers had caught sight of him through the dirty skylight, but Maltravers did not interrupt what he was doing. With a pair of tongs, he picked up one burning coal and held it close to

Chang's face, at the same time pinning him with an evil smile.

'Are you sure you don't want to change your mind, my dear fellow?'

Sam glanced hurriedly at Ann-li. He didn't want his friend to see her father being humiliated, or perhaps even tortured. But Ann-li was hunched in a corner of the roof, with her back to Sam.

Chang was staring at the red-hot coal and stammering with fear.

'I would like to, C-Colonel, because I am afraid, but I – I ca-cannot.'

Then Maltravers spoke words that filled Sam with horror.

'Chang, if you refuse to do what I am asking, you will oblige me to take your *own* daughter from you.' Blowing on the coal, he smiled at Chang. 'Yes. To help you see reason . . . we shall have to take your daughter away . . .'

Chang was shivering with fear. He darted for the door, but Dooley was too quick. He seized Chang by the neck, jerked him off the floor and held him, dangling like a puppet.

'Do not make me hurt you,' said Maltravers, ripping open Chang's robe and exposing his chest. He threatened him again with the glowing ember. Sam almost yelled out in rage. 'Just do as I ask,' taunted Maltravers. Chang was still gawping in horror at the burning coal. He tried to turn away, but Dooley's grip was vice-like, and Chang couldn't even get his feet on the floor.

Maltravers moved the hissing, glowing coal closer and closer to Chang's chest. Sam felt angry and helpless. He couldn't bear to watch any more. He slid over to Ann-li. They were just going back inside through the window when the night was filled with another howl of terror and pain. This time, Sam knew it was not a dog.

2

SEEN AND HEARD

On the face of it, Billy Chizzell and his mate Potts from Soho could have been brothers – same height, same light brown hair, same blue eyes, but that was where the similarities ended: Potts was lean and stringy, Billy was chubby. And their characters were completely different. Potts was streetwise and 'larky', whilst Billy, who was basically serious-minded, was a dreamer, coddled by his mum. He was trying to explain to Potts why he felt hurt, deceived.

'Mr Holmes has just disappeared, Potts, and Dr Watson won't do blooming anything. He wouldn't talk to me about it anyway.' Billy was convinced that with Potts's help, he could find Holmes. 'Listen,' he went on, 'it's dead simple. Nobody is even looking for him, so if we can find him, we'll be famous.' His head was full of dreams of glory. 'Think of the headlines – *"Young heroes locate Master Detective!"*'

Potts contemplated Billy's proposal. 'Billy, ol' cock,' he replied, smiling, 'you're orf your bleedin' chump!' Billy looked so disappointed that Potts felt bad. 'Nar . . . wot I mean is you ain't got nuffin' to go on. You'll *have* to consult the ol' doc.'

'He doesn't take me seriously. And anyway, *he* wouldn't know which way round to sit on a horse.'

'The trouble is, Billy, you ain't got no info.'

'Who's going to give me that then?' asked Billy. 'Not Dr Watson for certain.'

'A spy,' said Potts with a twisted grin.

'Don't get larky, Potts.'

'No I mean it, Billy. You need someone who has seen or 'eard somefin' that they don't p'raps realise is important until you come along. You then put all the pieces of the jigsaw togevver, and tell them that theirs is a crucial missin' bit of evidence, and 'ow you *know* – cos you 'ave the overall picture – that wot they *thought* was a totally useless bit of informashun is in fact . . . oh cobblers, I give up.'

'You're right though, Potts. That's exactly what we need – someone who's seen or heard something.' He stopped to think. 'Got it. I know who to go to.'

'Who?' said Potts.

'Edie! Why didn't I think of her before? She hears all sorts of things. We can go see her in the morning.'

Sam Wiggins had always been afraid of sleep – with sleep came nightmares – and always the moonlit chase: a faceless pursuer, Sam running for his life, trying to escape. Since the great fog, his restless nights were made even worse by an insistent, ghostly voice – the steely voice of Colonel Maltravers, saying, 'We shall take your daughter . . . we shall take your daughter.' Sam hadn't told poor Ann-Li what he had seen. Or even half of what he had heard. Nor did he know how to repay Chang and his family's kindness. He felt useless, unable to do anything at all. He wanted badly to help and hated not being able to. Nor could he get the awful pictures out of his mind: the massive Dooley, dangling Chang in the air; the evil Maltravers, threatening him with the burning coal, and then the voice – 'We shall take your daughter.' There was also the moment when Maltravers *might* have seen him; that made Sam shiver with fear. When he did eventually get to sleep, Maltravers and the phantom who pursued him through his dreams merged into one.

Sam had been on the wherry for a week. His job of looking after it for the Captain was nearly over, and everything had gone well. This was his sixth night on board and so far there hadn't been any problems. Only one to go. He lay on his bunk wrapped in a cosy blanket, trying to think of nice things, good things, to keep the horrible voice and the creepy memories at bay. He was warm, he'd eaten, and he was earning money. The fog had gone and the night was clear; through the round cabin window, Sam could see the moon. He allowed himself a rare moment of feeling contented. It was a mistake.

The wherry was swaying slightly with the current, but the movement that Sam felt now was more than that. He suspected that someone was on the gangplank: someone who had no right to be there. Sam eased himself off his bunk, and slowly to the floor. He picked up the short, sturdy club that the Captain had left him for protection. He had to move cautiously or he would give himself away. At the cabin door, which he had bolted before turning in, he listened. There was definitely someone out there. Close. He could hear them breathing. He could hear their fingers moving round the edges of the door, feeling for a way in. This was like one of his nightmares. Should he wait, and hope they would go away? Or do something? He raised the club, shot back the bolt, and whipped the door open. He half expected to see Colonel Maltravers, the ghastly pursuer of his dreams, but to his astonishment, a small, whey-faced child looked up at him and said quietly, 'I'm not breaking in, mister.'

'Oh no?'

'Not stealing, I mean. I'm just looking for somewhere to sleep.'

'Is that so, sonny?'

'Ay, it is. Honest.'

Sam lowered the club and looked hard at the kid, who was weather-beaten although his manner was mild, almost gentle. His voice was low and husky. Sam could tell he wasn't local.

'Where you from?'

'Up Lancashire way.'

'Where's your home?'

'I en't got no home.' The kid was shivering. He pulled his cap harder on to his head, as if it might make him warmer. 'Like I say, I just need a bed.'

'Long way to come for a bed,' remarked Sam. He felt inclined to help the kid, and was wondering how he might, when a loud, metallic clang nearby made them jump.

Next to the Captain's wherry, in among the factories and dockside buildings of a busy wharf, stood a disused warehouse. From the landing quay, a metal wall ladder climbed fifty feet, up to a trapdoor in a towering platform that jutted out from the front of the warehouse, out over the river. This trapdoor had been swung open, making a great hollow clang – metal on metal. Sam motioned the kid to keep quiet, and pointed. Two men were silhouetted against the moonlit sky. The smaller of the two was standing on the platform; the other – a colossal man – rose through the trapdoor with a large bundle on his shoulder – a sack. Sam had rarely seen such a big man: the last time was at Chang's, just over a week ago, when he had first set eyes on Dooley through the skylight. Even at a distance, in the moonlight, this looked very like him. The sack over his shoulder was moving. Struggling. Kicking. Shouting – a girl's voice. A hand lashed out. From within the sack there came a stifled cry, and then there was silence. Sam remembered again the steely voice: 'We shall take your daughter . . . we shall take your daughter.' It was Ann-Li. Ann-Li was in the sack – he was convinced of it. Colonel Maltravers had fulfilled his threat and taken her! The large man was Dooley – he was sure of it – the man with the scar on his cheek, and the smaller man had to be Maltravers. Maltravers unlocked a door into the warehouse, and both men went inside. The night was still again.

Sam couldn't look at the kid. He was trying to stay calm. 'You want a bed, eh?' he asked.

'Ay, please, mister.'

Sam now looked down at the would-be intruder. 'What's your name?'

'Simpson. Pat Simpson. Me mates call me Titch.'

Sam looked hard at the kid. He was tiny – he would have made a perfect chimney sweep's boy. 'How old are you, Titch?'

'Thirteen.'

'Oh yeah?'

'No, I am.' Titch was clearly frightened. 'I'm small for me age.'

Sam looked him straight in the eye. 'Well, big boy, you want to *earn* yourself a bed?' Titch looked cagey. 'I can't leave this boat,' said Sam, 'but if you take a message for me – not far – I can guarantee you a bed.' Titch nodded. Sam told him how to find Chang's Seamen's Hostel, and asked if he had ever seen a Chinaman.

'Ay, there are lots over in Liverpool.'

'Good. Ask for Mr Chang. Tell him Sam sent you.'

'Yeah?'

'That's me, yeah? And tell him Sam knows – listen carefully – Sam knows . . . *where they're keeping Ann-Li*.' Titch looked baffled. 'Those two men up there have got Mr Chang's daughter, Ann-Li,' Sam explained. 'Ann-Li's a friend of mine. Tell Mr Chang not to worry, and that I'll be round tomorrow, as soon as I'm finished here. All right? You *must* tell him not to do anything. Just wait for me. Yeah?'

'Yeah. What about the bed, then? Where am I gonna sleep?'

'Ann-Li's mum'll give you a bed – she don't understand much of the lingo, but she's a real nice lady. She'll take care of you. If there's a problem, come back here.'

'Thanks, mister,' said Titch, setting off down the gangplank. 'Bye.'

'Bye,' said Sam. He watched the small kid, who turned back and half waved to him. Sam could read people well – it had saved his skin more than once – and although he knew Titch intended to do as he asked, he also suspected that he was hiding something – and it wasn't just his age. He wasn't sure what, but he had an instinct.

* * *

37

By the hansom-cab rank outside Baker Street Railway Station, angelic little Edie McArdle was sitting on a rug on the pavement, selling small bunches of bedraggled herbs to the morning commuters. 'Herbs! Ha'p'ny a bunch!' she called sweetly. Potts couldn't imagine anyone less likely than this forlorn waif to help them find Sherlock Holmes. But he wasn't surprised – most of Billy's ideas were half-baked.

'You never give up, Billy, do you?' said Potts, smiling. It was true; Billy's head was always in the clouds. He never had his feet on the ground. And he never gave up! That was half his charm. Billy introduced them. 'Edie, this is my pal Potts.'

'Hallo, Potts,' she smiled. 'Would you be having another name?'

Potts was taken by the Irish lilt in her voice, but he was evasive about his name.

'Course I got anuvver name. But people call me Potts. Always 'ave.'

Billy knew that Potts's first name was Eli. But Potts didn't like it. So Billy didn't let on. Instead he said, 'Potts works for Jacky Dyke.'

Edie was impressed. 'Jacky Dyke?' she said. 'The King of the Silver Ring? Sure, I'll bet he's a character.'

'You'd bet right, Edie! And Mr Dyke'd give

you very favourable odds 'n all.'

The world of horse-racing was something Edie was rather scared of. There were famous stories in her family of a relation who had squandered everything he owned by betting on horses. He ended up gambling his wife away, so betting was strictly forbidden in the McArdle household! 'What do you do for him exactly?' she asked suspiciously.

'I'm a bookie's runner,' said Potts proudly, hooking his thumbs in his waistcoat and splaying his fingers.

'What does that mean?'

'Well I 'ave to go round the pubs collectin' bets, like.'

'And paying out, too,' added Billy. 'It can be blooming dangerous. He often has *loads* of cash on him. Don't you, Potts?'

'Quiet, Billy – everyone'll want some!' said Potts, putting a finger to his lips and pointing to his jacket pocket. Billy and Edie smiled. Potts enquired if Edie was selling any of her herbs today. She shrugged. Business was obviously not what it should have been.

'You wanna sprinkle some water on 'em,' quipped Potts, 'liven 'em up a bit.' In response, Potts noticed that Edie brought a bunch of rosemary really close to her face to examine it.

said he ought to be getting back to Mr Dyke. Billy said he'd join him, adding, 'Listen, Edie, that was really helpful. Thanks.'

'Any time, Billy. Sure, it's sweet of you to pop by. Bye, Potts. See you again, I hope.'

'For definite. Bye, Edie.'

As the two lads walked off down the Marylebone Road, they could still hear Edie's cry: 'Ha'p'ny a bunch. Rosemary! Only a ha'p'ny!' Potts was about to speak, when Billy stopped him. Rounding the corner into a smart mews he explained, 'You got to be real careful about what you say. She's got the most incredible hearing – that's why I thought we should go talk to her. It's like it makes up for what she can't see. She's going blind, Potts.'

'Yeah, I noticed,' said Potts, humbled. 'This tosh abaht a Chief, though, Billy. It's dopey.'

'It's not, Potts! It's the clue we're looking for. And you've got to believe her – Edie wouldn't make a thing like that up. Mr Holmes has gone down Limehouse, to the docks. No one else knows where he is, but now, *we* do. We nip down there, we find this Chief bloke, who's got to be some kind of boss. He tells us where my guv'nor is, and then we're famous, see?'

'The Chief, eh? Just like that?'

42

'Yeah,' said Billy. 'Just like that.' Potts remained unconvinced. 'What you waiting for, Potts?'

'The Chief, eh?' said Potts.

'Yes. The *Something* Chief.'

'Perhaps you could find me a couple of Red Indians 'n' all.'

Billy was too busy dreaming of glory to see the joke. 'Tell you what, Potts, tomorrow morning, early, I'm going to jump on the back of a hansom-cab, steal a ride down to Limehouse, and find Mr Holmes. You up for it?'

'I'm busy tomorrow,' said Potts. 'Mr Dyke.'

'Well, that's your problem,' said Billy, hiding his disappointment. '*I'm* going to Limehouse. To find Mr Holmes. And when I do, and I'm all famous, you won't half be sorry you weren't there!'

Sam hovered uncomfortably in the doorway of Chang's living-room. He could see blisters and burn-marks on Chang's neck and chest. He also observed a faded tattoo on Chang's left forearm. Mrs Chang bowed to Sam, and continued changing the dressings on her husband's wounds.

'Come in, Sam,' said Chang. 'We so glad to see you.' Chang winced with pain as his wife touched a particularly raw spot. Sam was embarrassed to be there. He felt he was intruding on something private, but Chang insisted. 'Come in. Your little friend who came last night told me you know where they got Ann-Li.'

'Yes, sir. She's in that big warehouse down by the docks. With the high crane. You know?'

'And the loading platform?'

'That's the one, sir. They've got Ann-li up top. It won't be easy to get 'er out.'

'Getting her out wouldn't be enough, anyway, Sam,' said Chang fearfully. 'These men stop at nothing. They would come for us again. Take my wife, our baby . . .' He indicated to Ann-li's little brother, asleep in a crib.

'They won't *hurt* Ann-Li though, sir.'

'Not yet, they won't,' muttered Chang. 'But I am running out of time. So is Ann-Li.'

'It's not in their interests to hurt her,' said Sam firmly.

'Aaah!' cried Chang in frustration. 'I just don't know what to do – now they got our lovely girl. Poor Ann-li.' Tears welled up in his eyes. Even though he knew the family well, Sam found the Changs' home strange, alien, but he envied Ann-Li a father who so obviously cared for her. Before his dad's death, he had felt part of a family himself. That seemed like years ago. Another life. His drifting thoughts were interrupted by Chang.

'Come here, Sam.'

Sam moved further into the room, but still felt as though he shouldn't really be there at all. Chang made him sit down.

'You don't know these people, Sam. The man in charge – who calls himself Colonel – he very clever . . .' Chang shook his head with bewilderment. His fingers strayed unconsciously to the faded tattoo on his arm. Sam was now close enough to see that it had once been a dragon – he had to stop himself staring at it. Chang tried to explain. 'The people he works for . . . they . . .' But, unable to find words terrible enough to describe his fear, he couldn't finish. He was rubbing the worn tattoo, as though he wanted to be rid of it, but what exactly did Chang mean? Had he once been a member of some gang? Is that what the tattoo signified? Whoever it was, they obviously still had some evil hold over him. Was Maltravers working for the same organisation?

Although he didn't fully understand, Sam desperately wanted to help. 'I'll think of something, Mr Chang, sir. You were good to me – you and Ann-li, and your wife – when no one else would look at me. I'll sort it out.'

'We have little time. They have given me three more days. Three days! And anyway, Sam, it is not for you to do. You must beware these men.'

'Don't worry; I won't do anything stupid, sir.' There was an awkward silence. 'Where's my mate? Did you take care of him?'

Chang said he was still asleep upstairs, and called his brother, Uncle Fu, to show Sam where.

As Sam was about to leave the room, Mrs Chang ran to him, took both his hands, and kissed them. Again, Sam was embarrassed. But he knew, with absolute certainty, that he would do anything he could to help the Changs get Ann-li back. Above all, he knew he would have to act fast.

3

THE 'SOMETHING' CHIEF

Ann-li felt sick with shock and fear. After her bewildering journey in the sack, she had no idea where she was. The room in which she was imprisoned was dark, and it was a long time before she could see properly. She was gagged, and she couldn't speak. She was cold and hungry. Ropes tethering her to an iron ring on the wall hurt her wrists and ankles, and the wooden floor which she was forced to sit or lie on was rough and splintery. She had lost all sense of time.

There was a peep-hole in the door. It was covered by a wooden shutter which was suddenly drawn to one side. Ann-li braced herself. A flickering light appeared, casting a thin ray into her 'cell'. Through the peep-hole she could just see Dooley's scarred face. Then Colonel Maltravers. Struggling to speak, Ann-li sat up.

Maltravers, unblinking, stared back. Then the shutter closed, and darkness returned.

In spite of his worries about how to help Ann-li, Sam felt good – the two silver sixpences the Captain had given him were clinking in his pocket. Leaving Chang's Seamen's Hostel, he led his new mate, Titch, down a sloping, cobbled lane, past a blacksmith shoeing a barge horse.

'Hi, Sam!' called the blacksmith. Sam waved.

'It were a bit spooky last night,' said the kid. 'Ann-li in the sack. Then at Chang's, all those people smoking. That sickly smell. And an old dosser frightened the daylights out of me.'

'Don't look 'em in the eyes.'

'Chang's missis was real nice, though, like you said. Fed me. Everything. It's terrible about Ann-li, innit?' Sam nodded. 'I had to sleep in her room. It were a bit odd. What you gonna do about it, Sam?'

'I'm thinking,' he replied. He had also been thinking about Titch, trying to puzzle him out. Sam was drawn to him, in spite of the feeling that he was hiding something.

A man rounded the corner at the bottom of the lane. Titch stopped, nervous. Sam told him not to worry – he knew the man, who touched his cap respectfully to them, and thanked Sam for a tip-off about a job as he passed. Sam was chuffed. Titch was impressed.

'Titch, are you planning to stop in these parts?'

'I en't got *no* plans,' said Titch.

'Cos if you was to lend me a hand, we could do a deal . . .'

'What deal?' asked Titch.

'Like . . . you help me out with Ann-li, and I'll show you where you can get some shut-eye.'

'Hey! That's fantastic. Thanks. That's great!' cried Titch.

Sam was a bit surprised by the enthusiasm of Titch's response, and felt he ought to warn him.

'It might get nasty, you know, Titch.'

'My life *is* nasty,' countered Titch.

'And we haven't got much time. We'll have to get on with it right away.'

'That's all right by me, Sam. It's not like I've got anything else on.'

Sam offered his hand. 'Deal, then?'

'Deal,' said Titch, and took it.

Billy Chizzell reached Limehouse early. He leaped off

the back of a hansom-cab and ran off, with the driver's curses ringing in his ears. The cab drivers hated the kids bumming lifts, but they all did it. It was dangerous and fun! Not to say quicker – it would have taken Billy well over an hour to walk it. He wished that Potts had been with him, but he plucked up courage, and started asking people for 'The Chief – the "Something" Chief'. A beggar-lad in a doorway shook his head sullenly. A knife-grinder threatened him. A couple of dockside workers simply laughed, and an old washerwoman thought he was taking the mickey – 'The Something Chief? Don't make me larf!' Billy hated to admit it to himself, but Potts had been right: The Chief was not going to be so easy to find as he had thought. And as for the fame he dreamed about – that was going to be much, much harder to come by. After a couple of hours of fruitless questioning, he was exhausted and fed up. But he had absolute faith in what Edie had told him: 'I heard Mr Holmes order a hansom to take him to "The Chief" – The *Something* Chief. In Limehouse.' So he ploughed on, determined to find either this Chief, or his master, Sherlock Holmes. Apart from anything else, he didn't want to lose face with Potts!

* * *

Sam and Titch turned on to the waterfront. It was crammed with people, wheeling and dealing, buying and selling. A tall-masted schooner carrying spices, that had docked earlier that morning, was being unloaded: the air was tangy with the smell of nutmeg and cinnamon – much nicer than the usual dockland odours! Sam steered Titch away from the crowds and into a little passage that ran between some low houses and a derelict pub. The top end of the passage was boarded up. It looked like a complete dead-end, but kneeling down, Sam opened a large flap in the bottom of the boarding.

'Home sweet home,' he said. 'In 'ere.'

Titch crawled through into the small back yard of the deserted pub. It was strewn with bits of furniture, crates and broken glass. The windows, too, were boarded. Titch's face fell: he had hoped for something better than this poky yard.

'Hang on,' said Sam, sensing his disappointment. He clambered up on to an old barrel and pulled on two planks, apparently fixed to the wall, that criss-crossed the boarding of a little outhouse window. The panel beneath the planks was hinged, and swung open like a door. Putting his finger to his lips, Sam ushered Titch into the pub. The entrance was so cleverly constructed that when they were both inside, Sam was able to close it, with the planks outside as before.

'Brilliant,' said Titch, though he didn't much like the dark, and kept close to Sam as he felt his way through to the main part of the pub.

'You'll get used to it, Titch. One rule – you have to talk real quiet.'

Titch gradually became aware of people sleeping – under the bar, on benches. Sam continued quietly, 'Quite a few people use this place, and we want to make sure the law don't cotton on. So we're all dead careful. In 'ere . . .' he guided Titch through a doorway into what *had* been the smoking lounge, 'this room ain't for sleeping.' Just enough light filtered through the cracks in the boarded window for them to see each other. 'Sit down,' said Sam, indicating a couple of cushions on the floor. He wanted to find out more about his new friend.

'Why did you come to London?'

'Got fed up with the life,' said Titch dismissively.

'What life was that, then?'

'Canals. Barges. Manchester Ship Canal mainly.'

'Why did you leave?'

'It were boring.' Titch shifted uncomfortably. 'I couldn't stand it no longer.'

'You didn't just leave, did you?'

'Quit asking questions,' said Titch, rather too loudly. Almost immediately there was another figure in the room, hissing at them to be quiet. He came out of the dark, looming up over the two boys, and Titch recognized the bearded, shabby figure of the old dosser who had scared him the night before at Chang's. He almost yelled out, but quick as a flash, Sam was on his feet, ushering the filthy tramp away.

'Sorry, mate. He's new. He'll be all right.'

'He'd better,' spat the old dosser.

Sam calmed him down, and the place was quiet again.

'He's the one I saw at Chang's,' said Titch.

'I wonder what he was doing there.'

'He were hanging about outside. Gave me a right scare.'

'Don't mind him,' said Sam. 'He's all spit and trousers. And anyway, he ain't been 'ere that long himself.' They settled back down again. Aware that his questioning had upset Titch, Sam said, 'Sorry about the questions, I'm just interested. There's no need to take on, you know, Titch. I'm in the same boat, meself.'

'Are you?' Sam hoped Titch might say more, and thought how vulnerable he seemed, but to his surprise,

Titch changed the subject. 'What is this place?'

'Was. Look.' Through a slit in the boarded window Sam pointed out an old pub sign, swaying gently, squeaking. Although the paint was peeling, Titch could just make out the strange, faded image of a bearded and turbaned maharajah, and below it, the words 'The East Indian Chief'. 'It's cos of the East India Docks,' Sam explained, 'where the boats come in from India – tea, spices, and stuff. And The Chief's a sort of joke, cos they don't have chiefs in India, they have rajahs. You know.'

Titch just said, 'India.'

'What about it?'

'My uncle's in India.'

'Army?'

'Harbour Master,' said Titch. 'Calcutta way.' Titch was still peering through the slit in the boards. Suddenly, he whispered urgently to Sam, 'Hey, take a look.'

Sam peered through the narrow gap in the boards. He could see a boy of about his own age, pudgy, quite well dressed, looking up at the ancient pub sign. The boy cried out, 'Oh no!' His face crumpled, and he looked as though he was going to burst into tears. Then, to Sam's astonishment and horror, he heard a voice he knew. It was the voice of the bald-headed man – Chang's torturer, Ann-li's kidnapper – the voice of Colonel Edmund Maltravers – the voice that haunted his sleep. It filled him with dread. Instinctively, Sam drew back from the slit in the panels. His mind was racing.

Outside in the street, Maltravers put a comforting hand on the boy's shoulder.

'You seem distressed, young man. What is your name?'

'Billy Chizzell, sir.'

'And what brings you here, young Billy Chizzell?' asked Maltravers kindly.

Billy started explaining about The Chief. How he had thought it was a person, and how it had turned out to be this derelict pub – The *East Indian Chief*. And how he didn't know *how* he was going to find his master, now.

'And what is your master's name?'

'Sherlock Holmes,' said Billy, miserably.

'Sherlock Holmes?' enquired Maltravers solicitously, closing in on Billy.

From behind the boarded window, Sam was still listening intently. 'Come on, Titch,' he said. 'We've got to help that boy! That man out there – he's the one that's got Ann-li. Quick!' And the two of them set off, back through the pub.

'Poor boy,' said Maltravers gently, as his arm slithered round Billy's shoulder. 'So it's Mr Holmes you are looking for?'

'Yes, sir.'

Maltravers nodded slowly. 'I see. Well, allow me to help you. Eh?'

'Yes, sir. Thank you, sir,' said Billy, relieved to be taken care of after his awful day. With apparent concern, Maltravers led him off along the dockside. When Sam and Titch emerged from the passage to the pub, there was no sign of either of them.

'We've got to find that lad,' said Sam. 'Goodness knows what that bloke'll do to 'im. They must have gone this way . . .' and he pointed along the quay. The two set off at a brisk trot, dodging and weaving through the crowds on the quayside. Glancing up a cramped alleyway, beyond a bunch of drunken sailors, Sam caught a glimpse of a bald head. 'Up here, Titch,' he cried. They set off up the murky alley in pursuit, but when they got close enough to see properly, Sam realised he was wrong. The bald head he had seen did not belong to Maltravers. They stopped. Defeated. Confused.

'What are we going to do, Sam?' panted Titch.

'I need to think,' Sam replied breathlessly, his hands

on his knees. Titch was already getting used to Sam, so he just waited. Suddenly, Sam stood upright. 'I'm a fool!' he said sharply to himself. 'A stupid fool! He'll take him to the warehouse. Where they've got Ann-li.' Taking a deep breath, they set off as fast as they could towards Ann-li's prison.

'Come on, Titch! If he gets that boy up there with Ann-li, they've both had it. *We've* had it!' Sam led them through a couple of short cuts. As they pelted round the corner on to the dockside and saw the warehouse, they were rewarded by the sight of Maltravers, his arm still around Billy's shoulder. 'Titch,' panted Billy, 'I'll distract him. You get the boy away, all right?'

'Sure!'

As they drew nearer, Sam could not keep images of Maltravers torturing Chang out of his mind. He also knew he would soon find out if Maltravers had actually seen him that night. Calling loudly, Sam ran up to Maltravers.

'Hey, mister. Mister!'

Maltravers's thin, mean face turned, and his still gaze fell on Sam. And Sam knew. He knew instantly that Maltravers recognized him. Maltravers's spine stiffened. His nostrils flared, as though he scented prey. The small sharp eyes glistened, fixing Sam with a basilisk glare. Sam froze. He had to summon all his courage and strength just to be able to speak. But it was essential for his plan to get and hold Maltravers's attention.

'I'm sorry, mister,' he stuttered, 'I think you dropped this.' His fingers shaking, Sam held up a threepenny piece. He could ill afford to give this money away, but he had to get Maltravers talking somehow, and it was all he had. Maltravers took the money, but not for one second did his eyes release their hold on Sam. They pinned the boy, whilst he turned the coin over and over, between thumb and bony finger. Sam noticed his unnaturally small, sharp, well-manicured nails, like claws. Maltravers drew breath, as if he was about to speak. Sam dreaded hearing again the steely voice, the voice of his nightmares.

'Be very careful, boy. You cannot know how dangerous it is for you to have me as your enemy. Take this back.' He offered Sam the coin. Sam did not want to touch Maltravers's dry skin. He held out his hand and Maltravers dropped the coin into it. Sam was relieved to have the money back, and so far his plan seemed to be working – Maltravers had removed his arm from Billy's shoulder, and Titch had managed to persuade Billy to edge discreetly away from him. Sam persevered.

'I don't know what you mean, sir. I'm sure this is yours. I saw you drop it.'

With the speed of a striking cobra, Maltravers's hand shot out and took Sam firmly by the lobe of his ear. Sam could feel the stubby claw, like nails digging in, forcing him sharply and painfully on to his toes.

'You think you are being clever, boy, but if you do not heed this warning – and it is the only warning I shall give you –' Maltravers drew very close to Sam and hissed into his stinging ear, '– it may cost you your life.'

Summoning all his nerve, Sam pushed Maltravers's hand away, and said, 'My life ain't worth living anyway, mister.'

Maltravers seemed to enjoy this bravado. 'To live badly, boy,' he breathed ominously, 'is better than not to live at all.'

Sam backed away, out of Maltravers's grasp. 'Rotten as my life is . . .' he said, showing much more courage than he felt, 'I wouldn't swap it for yours.' The moment the words were out, Sam knew he had gone too far, and he regretted it, but it was too late.

Maltravers did not move. He stood uncannily still, taking in every detail of his young foe, pinning Sam with unblinking eyes. The tip of his tongue appeared, sharp between his teeth, flickering as it moved slowly from one side of his mouth to the other. Then his lips tightened and, without so much as a word, he turned away. Passing Titch and Billy, he stopped and eyed each of them in turn. 'I hope, for your sakes, that I do not see *any* of you again,' he said. He put his hand on Billy's head, ruffled his hair in a friendly way, and added very quietly, 'Goodbye, young Billy. I trust you find Sherlock Holmes before I do.' Then he smiled, and slid away along the quayside.

They stood and watched, mesmerised by the venomous, hypnotic power of the man.

Billy was the first to speak. 'Wow!'

Titch was concerned for Sam. 'Are you all right?'

'Give me a second,' said Sam, who was still trembling.

'Wow!' said Billy again.

Titch turned to Billy. 'My name's Titch. That's Sam. It was 'im what saved yer.'

'Wow!' Billy repeated. It was all he could manage. He realised what a close shave he'd had. 'Thanks. Both of you. I mean . . . wow!'

Sam's mind was working fast. 'Listen, Billy. You're looking for Sherlock Holmes, right? Well, I think we might be able to help. And if you're game, there's . . . er . . . a little something . . . that you might be able to help *us* with.'

Titch smiled. He knew Sam was thinking of rescuing Ann-li. That meant taking on Maltravers. And Sam had referred to it as 'a little something'. Titch could hardly believe his ears! This Sam was quite a card!

The three of them stood for a moment, still under the spell of the evil Maltravers.

'Come on, you two,' said Sam, galvanising them. 'We've got a lot to talk about.'

4

THE EVIL PROFESSOR

On one of Maltravers's visits to Chang's Seamen's Hostel, Ann-li's father, in desperation, offered him a huge wad of money to release his captive daughter. Maltravers threatened to throw the money on the fire, taunting Chang, and laughing at his miserable pleading. He simply reminded him that the deadline was getting nearer – unless he did as he was asked, he would never see Ann-li again.

Poor Chang. Trying to go straight, he had run away to England, but the Dragons didn't like clan members who refused to carry out their orders, and the unforgiving past had caught up with Chang in the shape of Colonel Edmund Maltravers. And now, Maltravers had Ann-li. Chang felt powerless.

Taunting Chang, Maltravers merely repeated his original offer: if Chang assisted him in the kidnap of young white children for use in the slave markets of Bangkok, Bombay and New York, the Dragons would forgive him. Chang foolishly made no secret of his horror at this proposal – he was determined to leave his criminal past behind for the sake of his family. But Chang was trapped. In shame and despair, he buried his head in his hands. Colonel Maltravers slipped noiselessly out of the hostel, licking his lips with glee. Chang's helplessness amused him.

If anyone had noticed the small, bald-headed Maltravers moving along the waterfront, they could not have had any notion of the depths of cruelty and wickedness that inspired him and gave him pleasure. He disappeared suddenly between two buildings where there was no apparent thoroughfare. One minute he was there; the next, he was gone.

Sam was really concerned about time: they had two days left before Maltravers's deadline expired. But before he could plan in detail how they were going to get Ann-li out of the warehouse, he and Titch would have to 'recce' it. They would do that in the small

hours of the morning, so they turned in really e.
before it was dark.

Sam, as usual, found it difficult to sleep. He lay there
thinking about what was going on. He sensed that it
wasn't just a simple case of kidnap, that behind the
taking of Ann-li there were deeper motives, and large,
frightening organisations. Maltravers was now, openly,
their enemy, but neither of them were aware of the
extreme dangers towards which they were heading.
Had they known that they were being sucked into a
world of evil beyond even Sam's darkest nightmares,
they would have stayed, tucked up in the warmth and
relative safety, under the bar of The Chief.

When Billy arrived back safely at 221b Baker Street,
the alliance he had formed with Sam and Titch didn't
seem quite such a good idea. He only had to think of
Maltravers, and how nearly he had fallen into his
hands, and he got the shivers. The question was quite
simple; did he care enough about Mr Holmes, and the
chance of getting his name in the papers, to risk his
neck by going back to the Isle of Dogs? He really
did want to find his master, and he felt sorry for
Sam and Titch's friend, kidnapped by Maltravers. He
was impatient for something to be done to find

Holmes, but – he had to be honest with himself – he was frightened.

In the warmth of the kitchen, Billy waited for Dr Watson to come home, and chatted to Mrs Hudson while she prepared supper. Nothing much ever really happened at 221b when the Great Detective wasn't there, but this evening their cosy natter was interrupted by a knock at the door. Billy bounded up from the basement, and discovered Inspector Lestrade on the doorstep. Billy knew very well that if one of Scotland Yard's leading detectives came in person to 221b, there must be some dark reason indeed.

'Good afternoon, Master Chizzell.'

'Afternoon, Inspector,' Billy replied. 'Mr Holmes isn't here, I'm afraid. It's him you want, isn't it?'

'It was indeed Mr Holmes that I wished to see. But I took the precaution of preparing a letter for him, or, in the event of his absence, Dr Watson.'

Billy had to stop himself grabbing the envelope from Lestrade. But even when Lestrade gave it to him and left, all Billy could do was take it to the study and place it on the mantelpiece. Next to the pile of opened letters that Sherlock Holmes kept pinned to the shelf with a little Persian dagger, it sat there, tempting him. But to his great frustration, there was nothing more he dare do until Dr Watson came back from work and opened it. He was tearing his hair out by the time Watson arrived.

It was not until nearly seven that the weary doctor got back to Baker Street after a series of late house visits. His heart was heavy: he was convinced that Holmes's absence – of over two weeks now – could only be explained by his fixation with Professor Moriarty, or 'The Napoleon of Crime' as Holmes referred to him. For years, Holmes and Moriarty had been locked in combat – the evil Professor masterminding every major crime in London, and Holmes endeavouring to outwit him. Watson had warned his friend many times of the dangers of this obsession; Holmes, he feared, had ignored him as usual. Locked deep in these gloomy thoughts, Watson was taking his key from his overcoat pocket when, to his surprise, the front door of 221b was opened eagerly by Billy Chizzell.

'Evening, Doctor. I thought you'd like to know—'

'Ah, Billy. I've just left young Edie.'

This stopped Billy in his tracks. 'And?'

Watson explained that although Edie was suffering no pain, there was little he could do to save her failing eyesight. With luck and good care, he assured Billy, it would be some years before she was completely blind.

'It's not fair,' said Billy angrily.

'Nor is it, Billy. But she has a fine spirit. And those sisters of hers really look after her.' Billy said he would go round and see her. 'That would be kind,' said Watson, as he trudged up the stairs, failing to notice that Billy, unusually, was right behind him.

'Doctor, sir! There's a letter,' said Billy, following Watson into the study. 'There, sir!' Lestrade's letter stared at them from the study mantelpiece.

'Is it from Holmes?' cried Watson.

'No, sir. It's *for* him. Mr Lestrade brought it himself! He said you should open it if Mr Holmes wasn't here.'

Watson tore the letter open and, ignoring Billy, devoured the contents . . .

It is rumoured that Professor Moriarty is here, on one of his rare visits to this country. 'Moriarty!' cried Watson. 'I knew it!' The letter continued . . .

One of his chiefs of command – Colonel Edmund Maltravers – is currently active in Limehouse.

Watson gasped. The subject of a major public scandal, Edmund Maltravers had been thrown out of the army fifteen years previously on charges of bribery and corruption. He had since been linked with the infamous Malabar pirates of the Indian and South

China Seas, and was now a hardened, professional criminal whom the police had been quite unable to capture. They had not even come close. Watson resumed Lestrade's letter . . .

> *Maltravers is believed to be working for Moriarty in association with the notorious Dragon clan of Shanghai. It has always been difficult to pin crimes on Professor Moriarty himself, such is his cunning, but if we could damage Moriarty's organisation by apprehending Maltravers, it would be most gratifying. I trust we may rely on your services in the pursuit of this man, and remain yours . . .*

Watson lowered the letter.

'What does it say?' asked Billy, keen to know if Holmes had been located.

Watson did not even hear. His mind was racing. The Dragon clan was gaining a foothold in Limehouse, where – Watson noted – Maltravers was now active. The fact that Holmes had recently been studying the Dragons, whose members (he had informed Watson over breakfast) carry a unique tattoo, was a further coincidence that the Doctor could not ignore. According to Holmes, the Dragons were extending their criminal activities from drug-related crime into 'white slavery'. Watson pondered Moriarty's involvement: *his* crimes were usually of a grander order, Moriarty would not be interested in child kidnap for its own sake – he must have some deeper crooked motive. But this, added to the fact that on the very morning of his disappearance Holmes had been talking of the Professor's evil genius, confirmed Watson's fears that Holmes had gone underground in pursuit of his old enemy. Watson felt completely helpless. He suddenly noticed Billy, standing there, looking at him.

'Ah! Billy!' he exclaimed. 'I had no idea you were still there.'

'Is it about Mr Holmes, Doctor?'

'Indirectly. But I am afraid, Billy, that is no concern of yours.'

Billy was seething with frustration. 'What are you going to do, Dr Watson? You must do something!'

'At this moment, I do not know what anyone can do,' said Watson, returning the letter to its envelope. Billy couldn't believe it. He was on the point of turning on his heels and stalking out of the room, when Watson said, 'I can hear Holmes.'

Billy listened. 'He's not back, though, sir.'

'No,' said Watson. 'But I thought I heard him

playing his violin.' He rose and went into his friend's room. Billy stood by the door. He wasn't allowed in Holmes's private chambers, but he could see Holmes's violin, lying there, in the open case. There was, of course, no sign of its owner.

'My imagination,' breathed Watson, gazing at the neglected instrument – a Stradivarius of great beauty. Lying in its case, inert, unused, the varnish seemed duller. It looked almost dead. Watson stared at it for some time, silent, troubled. Billy felt uncomfortable – as though he was watching something private, something secret, some train of thought not intended for him. Watson shuddered, and closed the lid, walked past Billy into the study, and sat down again in his armchair.

Billy crept downstairs, embarrassed, disturbed, and angry that people were being so impassive. He could not rid his mind of the idea that Watson had been staring at the violin in its case as if it were a body in a coffin – Holmes's body. The fact that, *still*, nothing was being done to find Holmes really annoyed him. Did Dr Watson honestly imagine that Holmes was dead? Or what? Why was he doing nothing? Putting aside his disturbing fancies, Billy made up his mind, there and then, to get back to Limehouse as fast as possible in spite of his fear. With Sam and Titch's help, he would try once more to find his missing master.

When Watson was reading Lestrade's letter, Billy had heard the name Moriarty for the first time. But neither he, nor Sam, nor Titch had the slightest notion that they were about to enter a web of wickedness spun by the evil Professor himself.

5

ANN-LI'S
WAREHOUSE
PRISON

Early-morning mist rose from the freezing river. Crouching on the quayside, at the foot of the wall-ladder that ran up the face of the old warehouse, Titch shivered and waited and thought about 'Mr Big' – the nickname they had given Dooley: how strong he must be to have carried Ann-li up this ladder. Titch peered up. High above, in the dark, Sam was just visible, clinging to the topmost rungs, struggling to open the trapdoor.

Sam didn't have the power in his arms to lift the heavy trap. Twice he slipped and nearly lost his grip on the cold iron of the ladder. The fifty-foot drop to the quayside below did not look pretty, but he had to get the trap open. He manoeuvred himself round, so he had his back against the ladder. Hooking his heels over the highest rung possible, he tried to force the trapdoor up with his shoulders. It shifted a fraction, but he knew it was hopeless. He started down again. This was a real nuisance. Sam couldn't even *devise* a rescue plan if he couldn't get up on to the platform. When he got back down to the quayside, he was short of breath.

'It's no good,' he panted. 'I can't move it.'

'Don't worry. I can get on to the platform without using the trapdoor, if you want,' said Titch, pointing at two thick ropes hanging from the crane high on the warehouse roof. 'I'll nip up one of those.'

'You're daft!' said Sam.

'No. I'll make it on to the platform easy, but there's no way *I'll* be able to lift the trapdoor to let you up, so you'd better tell me what you need to know.'

Sam felt instinctively protective towards Titch. 'It's too dangerous, Titch.'

'If you want to find out where they've got Ann-li before that slimy Maltravers gets back, you ain't got much choice,' said Titch.

'You're right. So listen – all you do is find out two things: where they've got Ann-li, and if we can get on to the roof from the loading platform, using that old derrick on the other corner. Nothing else. You've got to be real careful, Titch. If we give the game away, we've

75

all had it – you, me, Ann-li, her dad, and her family.'

'Are *they* in danger 'n' all, then?' asked Titch.

Sam explained his theory. 'I reckon there's some*one* – or some gang – who's got something on Ann-li's dad – it's more than just them two – "Mr Big" and Maltravers.'

'What you gonna do?'

'I'm thinking. You ready?'

'Ay,' said Titch. But he didn't move.

'What's up, Titch?'

'Sam, d'you reckon Billy'll come back like he said?'

'My thinking is, that if he really wants to find Sherlock Holmes, he'll come,' said Sam. 'What d'*you* reckon, Titch?'

'He's dead keen.'

'He'll come, then. I wish we had some information for 'im.'

'Not 'alf. But we got our hands full right now. Give us a leg up, Sam.'

Sam made a crook with his hands, and lifted Titch easily till he had hold of one of the ropes.

'It's a bit big,' said Titch – he could barely get both hands round it – 'but I'll manage.' He gave it a pull to test it, and then he was off, his feet against the wall, leaning out backwards, and walking up it as easily as if he was strolling along the quayside. Sam couldn't believe his eyes.

On the platform, Titch paused to recover breath, then took a proper look at the warehouse. Directly in front of the trap there was a door into the warehouse; on either side of the door was a window. The far one was boarded; beneath the near one lay some planks that someone – presumably Dooley – had removed. Through the dirty glass came a dim, flickering light. Nervously, cautiously, Titch peered in. It was hard to see in the gloom, but he gradually made out a vast room. On the right side, there was a long row of doors into what looked like offices, and the dull light from a hurricane-lamp was coming through the open door of the nearest one. On the opposite side, a gallery overlooked the main body of the warehouse below, and along the side of this gallery, by the railings, there were disorderly piles of wooden pallets. At the far end of the room, Titch could just make out a stack of tea chests. The feel of the whole place made Titch uneasy. It was grim. There was no sign of Ann-li, but Titch soon spotted 'Mr Big'.

He was stripped to the waist, doing pull-ups on a beam, the light from the hurricane-lamp glinting on the bulging muscles of his arms. Titch could just make

out the great scar on Dooley's cheek as he raised himself very slowly till his chin was above the beam, then lowered himself till his arms were straight again. The power of the man was awesome. Slowly up. Hold. Slowly down. Hold. It was hypnotic. Then he stopped. He was completely still, hanging, listening, as though he had heard something. Abruptly, he dropped to the floor and moved very fast, straight for the window through which Titch was watching. Titch flattened himself against the wall. Dooley rubbed the pane clean with his hand and peered out. Then Titch heard him walking towards the door. Paralysed with fear, he heard the door opening. There was nowhere for Titch to hide. He had to force himself to run, and launch himself at the ropes. He nearly missed his hold, but just managed to hang on. He slid down quickly, to below the level of the platform, where he was out of sight. Hands burning, he trapped the rope between his feet, locked himself in position, and froze. Dooley was pacing the platform. His footsteps came closer. They stopped, a yard from Titch's head. If he looked over the edge, Dooley couldn't fail to see Titch. Nothing happened. The stillness and silence were unnerving. At last, Dooley moved away, and then on, round the platform. Eventually, Dooley's footsteps retreated and

Titch heard him close the door. He waited. Then he worked his way stealthily back up the rope and peered on to the platform. All clear.

Titch moved silently back to the window. Inside, he could see Dooley walking away from him, with the hurricane-lamp now in his hand. Near the far end, he stopped and banged on one of the doors, shouting, 'Oi! You! Wake up!' His speech was thick and hard to follow. He slid back bolts, top and bottom, slung the door open, and went in. Titch had to wait for some time before Dooley emerged, but he could just hear his voice. 'Go back to sleep,' he said. He then shut the door and re-bolted it. Titch nodded: it had to be where they were holding Ann-li.

Down below, Sam waited anxiously. He was rather surprised by himself: he had always been a solitary boy, and yet he had developed a sympathy with Titch, almost instantly. They got on. Titch made him feel good about himself, and he was amazed that this small, rather mysterious kid, about whom he knew so little, about whom he had certain suspicions even, had undertaken such a dangerous mission just to help him out. His thoughts were broken by the sound of footsteps. He nipped swiftly round the corner of the warehouse and took cover. From his hiding-place, he was stunned to see Maltravers emerging from the shadows. He wanted to warn Titch, but there was nothing he could do. He watched, helpless, as Maltravers began to climb the ladder.

High on the platform, Titch was unaware of the approaching danger. He had crawled under the window, past the trapdoor and the boarded-up window, to the far side of the platform, where a chain hung down from a derrick. Sam needed to know if they could use it to get on to the roof. Titch would have preferred a rope – the huge, oily chain looked slippery, but at least it felt secure. He was about to test-climb it when he heard a noise beneath him, from under the platform. Someone was mounting the ladder fast, and Titch was marooned on the wrong side of the platform. The ring of the iron rungs grew louder. Titch did what he could to conceal himself behind the chain, and held his breath. The trap began to open, and to his horror, he saw the gleaming scalp, the deep-set eyes and thin, cruel lips of Colonel Maltravers. Preoccupied, Maltravers opened the trap with speed and went straight into the warehouse without closing the trapdoor. Titch did not move. He strained to hear.

'Dooley!'

'Colonel!'

'Is the girl there?'

Dooley came running. 'Yes, Colonel.'

'Are you sure?'

'She-she's there,' stammered Dooley. ' 'Pon my honour, Colonel. I just checked.'

'It will be most unfortunate for *you* if she isn't.' Maltravers's voice was harsh and low. 'You haven't seen any kids snooping around?'

'No, Colonel.'

'Well, it will be most unfortunate for *them* if you do. Wretched, interfering kids. If I get my hands on them . . .'

Titch was tempted to nip through the trap and down the ladder, but Sam had been adamant he was not to risk giving the game away. He became aware of Dooley's voice, suddenly louder. 'Please, Colonel . . . don't do that.' He sounded as if he was in pain. 'Stop it!' growled Dooley. Titch wondered what Maltravers was doing to him. Titch couldn't understand why the big man didn't retaliate. Clearly, this giant, who could have crushed Maltravers easily if he had wanted to, was in the smaller man's power. Dominated by him. Frightened of him. 'Stop!' Dooley shouted. Then there was quiet.

The sound of footsteps moving towards the door

broke the strange mood. Titch froze. Dooley came out on to the platform, muttering darkly to himself, shut the trap, and re-entered the warehouse, closing the door. Able to breathe freely at last, Titch crossed the platform swiftly and silently. Heady with relief, he began to make his way back down the rope. Sam watched from below.

When Titch was about halfway down, a bit of paper worked its way out of his back pocket. It fluttered down and Sam tried to catch it, but it drifted into the river. Quickly, he lay on the quay, grabbed it and shook the water off. It was a photograph. Sepia. Battered. It showed a seafaring man with his arm around a little girl. The little girl looked like Titch. Sam stared at it in disbelief! A girl. Titch – a girl? He had always felt Titch was hiding something, but that had never crossed his mind! Suddenly he heard Titch's voice, whispering urgently.

'Give us a hand, Sam.'

Sam helped Titch down, asking anxiously, 'Are you all right?'

'I'm fine.'

'Are you sure?'

'What's the matter? Why you talking like that?' asked Titch, surprised by Sam's evident concern. Then, catching sight of the photograph in Sam's hand, 'Where d'yer get that?'

'It fell out your pocket jus' now.'

'It's my uncle,' said Titch, hurriedly. 'The Harbour Master what I told you about.'

Sam held the photograph out, hoping that Titch might offer him some further explanation, but Titch just took it and turned away. 'I don't like that place up there, Sam. It's creepy.' Titch's voice was low and husky.

Sam felt confused. 'It's got a nasty history,' he said, not really aware of what he was saying.

'What? Ghosts?'

'No. Convicts. For transportation. Down Under.'

'You just know people died in there,' said Titch quietly. 'Poor Ann-li.'

Sam said nothing. He couldn't take his eyes off Titch: the short hair, the wiry arms. Was that Titch's secret? Was Titch a girl?

'At least I found out where Ann-li is, Sam.'

'Good.'

'And we *can* get on the roof from the platform. There's a chain. It's greasy, but it'll do.'

Sam was confused. He didn't know what to think. He didn't know what to say. He needed time.

'Let's get back to The Chief, Titch. Thanks to you,

we know what we need. I can plan now,' he said. 'Come on.'

The pair made their way cautiously along the quay in silence, with Sam slightly ahead. He couldn't look Titch in the eye. Had he turned round, he would have seen that Titch was downcast, miserable. Their relationship, which had been so easy and close, now felt strained and uncomfortable. However, Sam had to concentrate on Ann-li. In fact, he found it easier to think about the rescue than about how he was going to cope with Titch – and apart from a few details, the rescue *plan* was now almost complete in his head.

6

SECOND THOUGHTS

'Herbs! Ha'p'ny a bunch!'

On this bright cold morning, regular Baker Street commuters recognised the words of her familiar cry, but to their surprise, Edie was sitting quietly on her rug. Barking lustily for her was Potts. 'Herbs! Fresh from the country! Fresh as dew!' He was busy sprinkling water on the unsold bunches of rosemary, sage and thyme, or running up to people to *show* them how lovely they were: 'Herbs – dirt cheap! Great value! Come on, you lucky people!'

Edie looked on, beaming. 'It's going really well today, Potts. You're a natural.'

'Glad to be of use, I'm sure,' said Potts, grinning. He enjoyed selling things, but his main reason for helping Edie was because he liked her. He had put on his favourite waistcoat in her honour – red, with thin black stripes – and a tired old bowler that his uncle had given him, which he only wore on special occasions. He liked Edie's fair skin and freckles, her fine auburn hair, and her sweet voice. He felt real anguish that she was losing her sight, and was intrigued by the other gifts she carried so lightly. He worked extra hard, just for her, so before lunch-time everything had been sold. A record!

'Sure, it's real sweet of you to give me a hand like this, Potts. Do you not have work of your own today?'

'I got some runnin' to do for Mr Dyke later, after the races. Takin' round the winnings, you know.' He plucked up courage and added, 'I got time to walk you 'ome, though. Would you like that?'

Edie was flattered. Boys didn't usually bother with her when they found out about her eyes. She smiled. 'I would love that,' she said. 'Come and meet my mum. And sure, I think Pop's there, today.'

Potts offered her his arm. 'Come on.' He helped her up, folded the rug and threw it over his shoulder. 'Got the dosh?'

'In the basket, Mr Potts, sir!'

As they left the station, a crossing-sweeper – a child of six or seven – offered to clean the road for them, but

Potts gave him short shrift – 'Get yerself a proper job, toerag!' – he wasn't going to have anyone else helping Edie today. He steered her carefully round the dirt and puddles, and helped her to dodge the hansom-cabs as they threaded their way across Baker Street.

'What does your pop *do*, Edie?'

'He likes to think of himself as an inventor, but his earning job is as a salesman like, on this newfangled thing they call the telephone. Do you know about it?'

'It'll never catch on, Edie. Tell him to invent a way of gettin' rid of all this 'orse dung!' He nodded at the piles of manure from the cab horses, shovelled into mounds in the gutter. 'Or why not invent drinkin' water. 'At's what London needs. *"Potts's Water! Water you can trust. Pots of it!"* Ha!'

Edie laughed. 'Will you be going to Limehouse this evening with Billy?' she asked.

'You been 'earing things?' said Potts cheekily.

Edie smiled. 'Only what Billy told me. He popped round last night to see how I was.'

'That was nice. And wot did he tell you?'

'Just that he *wants* you to go with him.'

'Yeah.'

'I bet I know what for,' said Edie.

'Bet you don't.'

'Well then let me see . . .' Edie stopped, took hold of Potts's hand and closed her eyes. She looked calm and peaceful, as though she was in a trance. She stood for a moment. 'The river . . . the river is important. I can see a boat.'

'Get on.'

'No, I can. I can see a little boat. And Mr Holmes is there . . .'

'Billy told you.'

'Sure, he didn't. Sometimes, I just get these pictures in my head. So . . . I can see two men as well. One of them is big. Very big. And . . . something I don't want to tell you.'

'Cos it's scary?'

'No. Cos you won't believe me.'

'Try me.'

'You won't believe me.'

'Course I'll believe you,' protested Potts.

'You won't.'

'I'll believe you, Edie! I promise I'll believe you.'

'All right,' said Edie, quietly. 'I can see a dragon.'

'I don't believe you,' said Potts with a grin.

'Ah, Potts, you're always larking, you.'

'I do me best. Come on.' But Edie wouldn't move. 'Hold on,' she said. 'I can hear Billy.'

'Wot?'

'I can hear him. He does this whistle when he's looking for me.'

'I can't see him nowhere,' said Potts, looking about.

'Just wait. He'll find us.'

After the 'recce' Sam and Titch caught up on a bit of rest. So by the time Sam sent Titch out to ask a few of his mates about Sherlock Holmes, they had only had time to talk about the rescue plan, which at least meant that Sam could avoid the business of the photograph. While Titch was out looking for information, Sam also had plenty to do – *his* task was to talk to the captain of the wherry. By the time he got to Chang's, Titch was waiting for him, disappointed to have nothing to report, and a bit concerned that Billy would not agree to help them if he was not getting any proper information about Holmes in return.

A tearful Mrs Chang informed them that Maltravers had paid another call that very morning. Her husband had actually gone away with him, and she was extremely worried about him and Ann-li. Nevertheless, she gave Sam and Titch something to eat and drink for lunch and, in the warm, they went through the details of Sam's plan.

'It's a brilliant plan,' said Titch, 'but for it to work, we 'ave to 'ave Billy, don't we?' Titch was right, the whole thing depended on Billy sticking to his part of the deal.

'He'll come,' said Sam reassuringly.

'I hope so,' said Titch. 'And he has to come tonight an' all. Doesn't he?'

Sam nodded. 'Yeah. He does. But he will, Titch. And who knows, he might even have his mate with him.'

'I hope so,' Titch repeated, trying to sound positive. 'What shall we do if he don't come, Sam?'

'I'm thinking.'

'Poor Ann-li.'

'We'll get her out somehow, Titch. We've got to.'

'How, though?' Before Sam replied, Titch knew what he was going to say.

'I'm thinking, Titch. I'm thinking.'

As Edie had predicted, Billy found her. He came tearing up the Marylebone Road.

'Hey! Get this, you two! I've just delivered a message for Dr Watson. Guess what it said.'

'Ask Edie,' said Potts. 'She'll tell you!'

'Sure, he doesn't take anything seriously, does he, Billy?' said Edie with a grin.

'Nothing, Edie. Not a thing. Listen. I've just been to Scotland Yard. With a note for Inspector Lestrade from the old doc. I reckon they'll be getting the police out to look for Mr Holmes. And I know why, because I took the liberty of taking a peek at a letter that was left for Mr Holmes yesterday. It was all about this Professor, who's a mastermind with an evil empire, and this really dangerous criminal who's working for him, at this very minute, in the Isle of Dogs, who I have actually met!'

'Get on!' said Potts.

'Straight up. And something about a gang called the Dragons.'

'Bloody *'ell*!' Potts was stunned.

'Didn't I tell you?' said Edie.

'What are you talking about?' asked Billy.

'I told Potts I could see a dragon, but he didn't believe me. Perhaps he will now. I don't know what it is you're about, Billy Chizzell, but it gives me the shivers.'

'Me, too,' said Potts.

'It sounds dangerous,' protested Edie. 'Anyways, it's not your business.'

'You're dead right,' said Potts. 'And I'm sorry I didn't believe you, Edie. On second thoughts, Billy, I don't fancy this.'

'*I'm* going, Potts. I did a deal.'

'And *they* said they'd 'elp you. 'Ave they?'

'How do I know if I don't go back? They might know exactly where Mr Holmes is by now. *They* tell us. *We* tell Inspector Lestrade. *They* catch this Prof chap and his sidekick. And *we're* famous.'

'Will you belt up wiv your flippin' fame?'

'Oh come on, Potts. It'll be exciting!'

'What?!? Mr H is missin'. You're on about a mastermind and an evil Prof. Edie's talkin' about big blokes and dragons. And you're goin' down to Limehouse just to stick yer 'ead in the dragon's mouth?!? You're a few violets short of a bunch, you are!'

'Well,' said Billy, 'I'll be coming for you at Mr Dyke's at the end of the afternoon. And if you let me down, and let Mr Holmes down, and the whole of Scotland *Yard*, I'll . . . I'll go on my own! That's what. And you won't like it when I'm famous and you're not! I'm coming for you. So that's that. All right?' And he stomped off across the road, nearly colliding with two soldiers on horseback. Potts was sullen.

'What are you going to do?' said Edie.

'I don't know,' said Potts. 'Let's talk about sumfin' else.' But neither of them felt much like talking at all now, so they strolled on in silence. For a while Potts felt bad about Billy, but much as he liked him, his mate never really understood what was going on right underneath his nose till it was too late. He was a dreamer. Potts turned to Edie.

'I don't suppose you can read the future 'n' all, can you, Edie?'

'I'd do it for you if I could, Potts, but it doesn't work like that.'

'No. I didn't fink it would, somehow.'

'Sorry.'

They turned into Lisson Grove, where Edie and her family lived in one of several tenement buildings that were so overcrowded they were known as the 'rookeries'.

'Come up and meet everyone, Potts. Sure, it'd cheer you up.'

'Anuvver time thanks, Edie. I need to fink fings out. Will you be all right from 'ere?'

'Sure I will. Thanks, Potts. You've been sweet. Bye.'

'Bye. Take care, now.'

'*You* take care,' said Edie meaningfully.

Potts's day had turned sour. He didn't really give a toss about Mr Holmes or Inspector Lestrade. He didn't want to go near the Isle of Dogs. He didn't like the sound of Moriarty or the Dragons. At the same time, he didn't want to let Billy down. The truth was, although he didn't like to admit it to himself, he was scared. Petrified.

Ann-li couldn't move at all; the ropes binding her were too tight and it was bitterly cold. She had to wriggle her fingers and toes to stop them going numb. The only real relief was when Dooley untied her gag at feeding time. Even then, Dooley didn't allow Ann-li to feed herself. His enormous fingers broke the hunks of bread and bits of cheese and put them slowly in Ann-li's mouth. Strangely, Ann-li wasn't frightened by him. But Maltravers terrified her: he was without feeling, dead inside. Ann-li often heard him abusing Dooley, berating him for his slowness and dull speech. She nurtured the fantasy that Dooley would rise up against Maltravers one day because of the way he treated him, but he never did. Once, he raised his voice. 'I don't like it, Colonel. It's wrong!' he shouted, but Maltravers hissed something at him, and he didn't speak again.

Through the indistinguishable days and nights Ann-li tried to puzzle out why she had been kidnapped. The family had left Shanghai for England to get away from something, but it obviously hadn't done much good. She suspected that this 'something' had to do with her

father's past, that it related to the dragon tattoo that he was always trying to scrub off his arm. She loved her father, and hated the notion that he had ever been a criminal. What had he done, so terrible, that these men were prepared to go to such lengths to maintain a hold over him? What did they want him to do now?

Ann-li lay in her dark and lonely world, longing to be back home in the warm, with her mum and dad, her uncle and her baby brother. Once, when she heard Maltravers asking Dooley if he'd seen any kids hanging about, she wondered if Sam might come to her rescue. But she didn't really believe he would. How could he? 'No one even knows where I am,' she said to herself. As the cold hours went slowly by, her friends and family seemed more and more like figures from a dream, and it seemed less and less likely that she would ever see any of them again.

7

WAITING

The dockside bustle of the day was over. Apart from a party of drunken dock-workers and a rag-picker sifting through piles of rubbish, there appeared to be no one but the rats. But in a doorway, behind a carefully arranged pile of packing-cases, Sam and Titch had hidden themselves in such a way that they had a perfect view of the warehouse. They were waiting for Billy, hoping that he would come. They were quiet and tense. And pessimistic.

'He's not coming, is he?' said Sam.

Titch tried to cheer him up. 'Well, he's not here yet.'

'He said he'd be back by dusk. The boats are ready. Chang's ready – he didn't look in very good shape when he came back this afternoon, did he?'

'Not really. D'you think Billy's chickened out?'

Sam nodded. After a moment's thought, he took a look in the direction of the warehouse. 'Maltravers is still inside, isn't he?'

'Ay.'

'Well, we can't get Ann-li out while he's around, anyway.' Sam was right: there was nothing they could do until the Colonel had gone. He settled back, brooding. Here, at last, was an opportunity for him to talk to Titch about the awkward business of the girl in the photograph.

To his surprise, Titch suddenly said, 'Did your family kick you out, then?' Sam was taken aback. He felt that *he* should be asking the questions.

'I got fed up with my new dad,' he said tersely.

'What happened to yer old one?' asked Titch.

Sam swallowed. 'He was killed. Fighting.'

'Sorry,' said Titch.

'For King and Country,' said Sam with pride, but Titch didn't understand.

'For what?'

'He was a soldier. He was killed at Khartoum.'

'Where's that?'

'You never heard of Gordon of Khartoum?'

'No.'

'It's in the Sudan.'

Titch still didn't understand. Sam was upset, and wanted to say that he had loved his dad, and missed him desperately, that sometimes he felt angry with him for having been killed, but he couldn't speak. He felt on the verge of tears, but didn't want Titch to see him crying. All he could manage was 'He was nice, my dad. I was proud of him, being a soldier and that. He wasn't afraid of anything.' He wiped his nose with the back of his hand.

'What about your mum?' asked Titch.

'She was all right till this new bloke come along. They run a workhouse together now, Enfield way. He didn't like me. He . . .' Sam still had a lump in his throat from thinking about his dad. 'He . . . "pushed me around". So I quit.'

'I get yer,' said Titch. 'Sorry.' And to take the pressure off Sam, Titch looked out at the warehouse. There was nothing happening. And with Titch looking away from him, Sam found it easier to control himself. After a moment, he said, 'It's worse for you, though, ain't it, Titch?'

Titch didn't move. 'What d'you mean?'

Sam's throat felt dry. 'Titch, who's the girl in your photograph?'

Titch didn't reply.

'There's no point in trying to hide the fact, Titch. It don't bother me if you . . . you know . . .' He petered out. 'Titch, just tell me. Who's the girl?'

Titch took the photograph out and looked at it. 'This is my uncle what I told you about.'

'Really?' said Sam.

'And that's my sister,' added Titch quietly.

Sam drew his chin in, in disbelief. 'Why d'you keep a picture of her?'

Titch shrugged.

'Titch . . .' said Sam. Titch tensed. 'I just told you about my dad. I've never talked to anyone about my dad. Not never.'

Titch was silent, but Sam didn't speak. Eventually Titch turned to him and said, 'You'll kick me out.'

'I won't.'

'Promise?'

'Course. We're . . . mates . . . ain't we?'

Titch shifted uncomfortably. 'Well, it *is* my uncle – in the picture – and with him – with him – it's me . . .' Titch gulped. 'The girl, I mean.'

'I thought so,' said Sam. There was another moment of uneasy silence, then he added, 'Well – you're not like any girl I ever met. In a nice way, I mean. Titch . . . what happened?'

Titch was pale. Looking down. A sudden intake of breath made her shudder. 'I ran away cos of my boss. On the canals.' Titch stopped, unable to go on.

'Why?'

'Well, he weren't just my boss. He were my dad. My proper dad.' Titch's voice dropped to a whisper. 'And I didn't like the way he treated me.' Sam was shocked. Titch continued. 'I thought . . . I thought I might kill him . . . so I did what you did. I left.'

'You poor thing,' said Sam. He was stunned. '*I'd* kill 'im if I had the chance.'

'Thanks,' said Titch.

They looked at each other. They had shared secrets. They had not been hurt. In fact, they felt closer. Briefly they forgot where they were, and what they were there for.

The Colonel held Ann-li in his cold stare. Behind Maltravers stood Dooley, huge and silent. The Colonel was talking. Quietly. Reasonably. His tuneless voice was hypnotic, telling Ann-li about her father. About his criminal past. What Ann-li learned was so awful that the poor girl began to think the dark solitude of her imprisonment had been preferable.

'Your father will never be able to hide from me. Do

you understand, you foolish girl? Never.' Ann-li managed to nod. 'Never forget what I have told you – your father either cooperates, or he will be . . . eliminated. And so will you. Tomorrow morning.' Smiling, Maltravers rose and left Ann-li's cell. Dooley closed and bolted the door. Until now, Ann-li had managed not to cry, but alone again, gagged, tied hand and foot, in near total darkness, she could feel her eyes burning.

'Dooley!' Maltravers summoned the huge man, who came meekly at his command. 'I shall have to leave soon. Professor Moriarty does not like to be kept waiting. Keep your eyes open, you halfwit. You are as disposable as the kid.'

'Hey, look!' said Titch suddenly. They both peered up at the platform. Dooley was holding the trap open, as Maltravers began to descend the ladder. 'I don't like the look of that Colonel bloke, do you?'

'He's scary, ain't he, Titch?'

'Mr Big is *dead* scared of 'im. You should 'ave 'eard 'im when I was up there.'

'What happened?' asked Sam.

'The Colonel were that foul to 'im, I thought he'd put one on him. But he didn't. He just took it. It were weird.' They watched as Maltravers reached the quayside. 'I feel dead sorry for Ann-li,' said Titch. 'I'm glad it's not me in there.'

'Not 'arf.'

Maltravers looked furtively about. His shining, skull-like head and bony white face, his piercing, unblinking eyes, his reptilian habit of licking his thin lips, all added to the impression that he was coiled inside like a snake, waiting to strike. Swiftly and silently he slipped round the side of the building.

Dooley closed the trapdoor and disappeared into the warehouse. Sam and Titch settled back. With Maltravers gone, the coast was clear at last. But as there was still no sign of Billy, all they could do was wait.

Titch felt wretched. People had often mistaken her for a boy, long before she had made the decision to run away, but now her secret was out, she felt vulnerable. 'Sam, you won't tell, will you?' she asked.

'Course not, Titch. I won't tell no one.'

Titch felt a surge of gratitude. Surprisingly, it was also a relief that someone knew, although Sam was quiet now, remote; but he was like that. Still feeling the need for contact, Titch asked, 'What can we do for Ann-li if Billy don't turn up?'

'That's what I'm thinking.' Sam was distant, locked

in thought. 'I was sure he'd come.'

'I thought so, too,' said Titch. She was confident that Sam would come up with something.

In silence they waited. As the evening turned colder, a light mist began to form.

Dr Watson sat by Edie's bedside, holding her hand. When she had suddenly fallen ill and lapsed into a fever, muttering incoherently, the family were worried. The eldest of her three sisters had run round to Baker Street to ask Dr Watson to come by. He was touched by the closeness of these girls, and the affection they had for Edie, the baby of the family. He brought her temperature down and made her comfortable.

He was happy to sit and watch her, bathe her forehead and keep her cool. Grasping his hand hard, she talked of ropes and chains, of falling, of drowning. It seemed to Watson that Edie was not exactly ill, but in the grip of something, and he was intrigued by the unusual nature of her condition. Being the kind doctor that he was, he listened for as long as he could, until his late appointment with Inspector Lestrade obliged him to leave for Scotland Yard.

* * *

As they sat waiting for Billy to arrive, Sam found himself thinking of Mr Big, and the repellent Maltravers, who held Ann-li and the whole Chang family in his evil grasp. Titch could see Sam was preoccupied, and kept quiet. Their dejected mood was interrupted by a noise from the dockside.

'Hey, Sam! It's that old dosser.' The tramp was hissing, shooing someone away, waving his arms in the air, furious, frantic. Titch suddenly realised who he was shouting at. 'Stone me! It's Billy. And guess what, he's got someone with him! His mate! I don't believe it. They're 'ere!'

But next moment, they were gone – legging it round the corner to get away from the old dosser, who was left raving at thin air.

'I shan't be a mo',' said Sam, nipping out of the hidey-hole.

The old dosser drifted away, cursing, and it seemed an age to Titch before Sam returned. The sky had darkened. When Sam finally got back, he had Billy and his mate with him.

'Great!' said Titch. 'You made it!'

'Sorry I'm late,' said Billy. 'Potts had a steward's enquiry.'

'Last race, Newmarket,' said Potts, and added with a

touch of pride, 'I'm a bookie's runner.'

'Fancy that!' said Titch, impressed.

'At least you're here,' said Sam. He shook Potts warmly by the hand, and introduced Titch. 'Now . . . we should get a shift on. Billy, you're staying here with me. Potts, you're going with Titch. He'll tell you what to do.' It felt odd, calling Titch 'he'. 'You clear, Titch?'

'Sure am.'

'Well then, get things moving. Good luck. See you later.'

Titch was standing close to Sam, and said quietly, 'Be careful.'

'And you,' replied Sam instantly.

'Come on, Potts,' said Titch, and the two of them slipped away.

Sam turned to Billy. 'I got to be honest with you, Billy, we've made a few enquiries about Mr Holmes, but we ain't got nowhere. We've been a bit busy with Ann-li 'n' that, but if everything goes according to plan tonight, we'll have another look for Mr Holmes tomorrow. All right?'

'All right.'

'If he's around here, we'll find him for you. I guarantee. It's just a question of time. Here. Grab these.' He gave Billy a small bag of pebbles. 'Stick 'em in your jacket pocket.'

'What are they for?'

'I'll tell you in a minute. Give me an 'and with this rope,' said Sam, indicating a huge length of rope lying on the floor. Billy helped coil and place the rope round Sam's shoulders. 'Time to go then. Ready?'

'What are we gonna do?' Billy asked.

'See that big building?'

'Yeah.'

'We're going up on to the roof.'

'You're kidding.'

'You'll love it. Come on.'

And they moved away through the fine mist and darkness, towards the warehouse.

8

ALL SET

Ann-li's baby brother lay screaming in his crib. Mrs Chang was aware of her son's distress, but she was numb with her own pain. Her husband, Chang, who was sitting by her on the edge of the bed, was trying to comfort her, repeating the words . . .

'We will get away from this place. Make better life. We will get away . . .'

Mrs Chang shook her head. 'But how? How can we? We never get away from these people.'

'I *trust* this friend of Ann-li's. He means what he says. I really think they will come. And they will help us to get away.'

'Sam and Titch cannot defeat that man Maltravers,' Mrs Chang insisted. 'I hate him. If he comes here again—' She broke off, sensing someone at the door. 'That's him . . .' she whimpered as the handle of the door began to turn, '. . . it's him. He's there!'

Chang got up and moved hesitantly towards the door. 'Yes?' he said loudly, trying to hide the fear in his voice. The thought of having to deal with Maltravers again made him ache with misery.

Slowly, as the door began to open, Mrs Chang rose and clung to her husband in terror. When Titch's head appeared round the door, she was so relieved, she nearly burst into laughter.

'Ah, Titch,' said Chang. 'It's you. Thank God.'

'I got a friend with me 'n' all. Sam sent us,' said Titch. 'You all ready?'

Chang turned to his wife. 'I told you Sam could be relied on, didn't I?'

Titch and Potts stood and watched as Mrs Chang turned her attention to comforting her baby. When he was calmer Chang turned to them and nodded. 'I just fetch my brother, Titch, then . . . we ready.'

'Good. Cos it's time to go.'

'Where does Sam want you to take us?'

'Don't worry. Sam's got it really well worked out. It's somewhere nice and comfy – a boat. You'll like it.'

* * *

Inspector Lestrade was a hardworking policeman, and a good, conscientious man. He sat at his desk in Scotland Yard contemplating the seemingly insoluble task of apprehending Colonel Maltravers, and the less urgent but equally difficult problem of finding Sherlock Holmes. Lestrade and his men had conducted a series of door-to-door investigations in the Limehouse area, and contacted all known informants, but they were no closer to locating either the elusive Maltravers or the Great Detective than ever. 'I am completely at a loss, Dr Watson. We can find not so much as a whisper of either of them.'

Watson had warned Lestrade that Holmes would be hard to trace, advancing his theory that Holmes would have gone underground, and would of course be in disguise. Standard enquiries, he insisted, would be a waste of time. The problem was, neither of them had any idea what else to do.

'Do you know where *Maltravers* is?' enquired Watson.

Lestrade shifted uncomfortably. 'He is very elusive. We had a man working under cover – the very one who first alerted us to Maltravers's presence here. He *was* helping us . . . but he disappeared. His body was washed up on the Isle of Dogs. This is a dangerous business, Dr Watson. Since that time we have found no trace of Maltravers.'

Watson stroked his moustache thoughtfully. After some time, he said, 'Lestrade, let us consider Moriarty's motives. I am convinced that if he *is* involved, his main interest will not be this wretched kidnapping of children. He will have some greater motive.' After a moment's reflection he added, 'By the way, what happens to these poor children?'

'There is a demand in some countries for children. For work in mines, maybe. For adoption if they are lucky. For a much less pleasant fate if they are not . . .' His voice drifted away.

'For some other kind of work, d'you mean?' quizzed Watson.

'It is referred to by the criminal fraternity as "white slavery".'

'Slave labour, do you mean?'

'Some people would call it that,' replied Lestrade ominously. 'I would call it abuse.'

Watson paled. He was shocked and angry. 'If you mean what I think, Lestrade, I cannot believe there are men capable of . . .' he struggled to find the words, 'capable of ill-treating young children in such a way.'

'The sad truth, Dr Watson, if the evidence of my

work is to be believed, is that men are capable of much worse things than you and I can conceive of, even in the darkest corners of our minds. This man Maltravers is, by all accounts, quite without feeling, beyond the reach of compassion or remorse. One can at least comprehend what drives a criminal like Professor Moriarty.'

'Power,' said Watson.

'Yes. Power. And the desire to fulfil a perverted genius, as Mr Holmes has often commented. But a man like Maltravers, one cannot fathom. The list of crimes for which he is wanted would turn your blood to ice. There are those who enjoy cruelty for its own sake.'

'What are we going to do, Lestrade?'

'I confess, Dr Watson, I do not know.'

The two men sat in frustrated and defeated silence. In the face of the threat posed by Moriarty and Maltravers, their good intentions were not enough. And they knew it.

Not far away from the current centre of Professor Moriarty's operations was a superbly fitted out railway-carriage. Moriarty was making skilled use of the fast-growing railway network, moving around anonymously, in his own private train. In a quiet siding near Farringdon Station, in great luxury, sat the very man so eagerly sought by Inspector Lestrade: Colonel Edmund Maltravers. Opposite him, his elbows resting on the rounded arms of a large leather armchair, sat Professor Moriarty himself. His hands met, cathedral-like, finger on spindly finger, thumb on thumb. His long, thin body gave an impression of complete relaxation, but his mind was clearly attentive, ready to pounce.

'Maltravers, answer me these questions.' As he grilled Maltravers, Moriarty's head moved slowly backwards and forwards, his large domed forehead seeming, as it moved, to be weighing issues of great significance. His questions focused on the 'white slave' operation he had asked Maltravers to put in place. Maltravers answered with absolute assurance – his manner was dispassionate and workmanlike – until the Professor had in his mind a picture of a nationwide network of operatives – London, Bristol, Liverpool, Newcastle – ready to provide him with his cargo of kidnapped children at a moment's notice. The tentacles of this organisation reached out into Europe, and as far afield as Asia.

'Good.' Moriarty's eyes hooded over. Maltravers knew better than to speak. He leaned back deep into his chair and waited. Slowly, Moriarty's eyelids opened to reveal the pallid depth of his light grey eyes. 'For now, we will do nothing. Things are in place. That is all I needed to know.'

'You have only to say the word, sir.'

'Good. I am pleased. The time is not yet, but it will come. And soon. Good.' Moriarty valued efficient work from his lieutenants; with failure he was merciless.

'Do you have any use for this girl we are holding hostage?' asked Maltravers.

'I do not concern myself with daily operations. Deal with it yourself.'

To Maltravers this meant only one thing. If Chang could not be persuaded, and that seemed unlikely, he would have to get rid of Ann-li. And the sooner the better.

A fine, cold mist veiled a crescent moon. In its gentle light, Sam and Billy climbed the ropes up to the warehouse platform without difficulty. They crawled beneath the unboarded window and past the door into Ann-li's prison, but when they reached the chain hanging down from the derrick, things got tricky. The huge links were oily, which made it difficult to get a good grip – Titch's fears had been well-founded. Sam managed to struggle up to the roof, but Billy was nervous, and his hands kept slipping. When he was nearly at the top, a good thirty feet above the platform, he looked down, but couldn't take his eyes off the mist drifting over the swirling river far below.

'Come on, Billy.'

Sam leaned over the edge of the warehouse roof and offered his hand, but Billy's look was fixed away from him. 'Billy!' he said sternly.

'My head's gone all funny, Sam. I can't move.'

'Don't look down.'

'I'm trying.'

'Look at me,' commanded Sam. Billy forced himself to look up. He was white with vertigo. 'Take my hand.'

But even when Sam shook his hand at him, Billy did not dare let go of the chain. He kept repeating, 'I'm going to fall.'

Swiftly, Sam leaned out, dangerously far, over the edge of the warehouse roof, and grabbed Billy's collar. 'Just push with your legs, all right? Now.'

Billy pushed, and with one mighty heave, and a deal of desperate scrabbling, Sam dragged him on to the roof. They lay there, panting with relief, trying to get their breath back.

'Thanks, Sam. That was foul. Everything was swimming.'

'You'll be all right, now. Just don't look down.'

'What's weird is, I sort of wanted to let go. You think it'll be nice, you know, and you'll just float down.'

'Well don't give it a try. Cos you won't. Listen, we'd best get on. When you're feeling up to it, go over the back there and have a look at that old fire escape in the far corner, cos that's *your* way down. And see if you can find anything to whack the roof with – an old stick or an iron bar. Anything. I'll fix this rope.'

Sam needed to be able to get down easily from the roof to the platform, which was why he and Titch had decided he should bring the rope, which the captain of the wherry had kindly provided. He set to work. Billy rejoined him as he was tying it off above the pulley on the derrick.

'That ought to make life a bit easier,' Sam said, ensuring that the knot was secure. 'How d'you get on, Billy?'

'The fire escape looks pretty rickety, but reckon I can cope if I don't lose my nerve again. And I found this chunk of wood.'

'That's lucky. We're ready, then. Keep your eyes peeled over there, in that direction.' Sam pointed downstream into the darkness. 'Titch and Potts were taking the Changs down that way – they should be safe by now. Titch might even be on the way. We just have to hope this mist don't get any thicker, or we shan't be able to see Potts's signal. We can't do anything till we get that. So while we've got some time to kill I'll fill you in on the rest of the plan.' They settled down to wait.

When Titch and Potts had delivered the Changs to their secret destination – the Captain's wherry – they were ready for the next stage of Sam's plan. Titch led Potts to a small rowing-boat moored close by. Potts just stared at it. 'What's the matter?' asked Titch.

Potts had gone pale – spooked by the accuracy of Edie's prediction. What had she said? 'The river is important. I see a boat.' If she was right about the boat, Potts was thinking, what about dragons?

'It's not far,' Titch went on. 'It'll be quite tough for me rowing up there, cos of the tide. But on the way back, it should be a doddle. And if things go according to plan, I won't be alone, then!'

'Bleedin' big *if*, innit?'

'I don't reckon it is, no. I think Sam's plan is brilliant.'

'Aincher scared?'

'I'd be happier doin' your bit. Keeping an eye on the Changs won't be dangerous, will it? Sending signals won't be either. That's all you've got to do. But I don't *mind* doin' the rowin'. I'm used to boats.'

'Kosher.' Potts was impressed.

'And Sam and Billy are doing the *really* dangerous bit.' Potts had no answer to that. Titch slid into the boat. 'Hand me the rugs. And that bag of stones – Sam said they might come in handy.'

'Wot for?' asked Potts.

'I don't know. But Sam's got things worked out to the letter,' said Titch, putting them in the stern. Potts handed the oars down, one at a time, helping place them in the rowlocks. 'Are you clear what you have to do, Potts?'

'Yeah.'

'Have you got the lamp?'

'Yeah.'

'Throw me the rope then. And give me a shove off.'

Potts untied the mooring rope, tossed it into the bows, and gave the boat a push with his foot.

'Good luck, Titch.'

The small boat slid away from the muddy bank and started upstream towards the warehouse. Potts watched as Titch rowed briskly away. He watched until Titch was almost out of sight, then began to track his way along the bank. All he had to do, before he made his way back to the Changs, was make two signals with the lamp Titch had given him. He was relieved to be doing the safest part of the rescue, but at the same time, a bit of him was envious that he was not going to be really involved.

'I'm getting worried, Sam,' said Billy, blowing on his fingers. 'I wish Potts's signal'd come. It's getting right parky up here.'

'It'll come.'

'I hope you know what you're doing, Sam.'

'I've worked it out.'

'So you keep saying.'

'Well, I have.'

'What if something goes wrong?'

'It probably will at some point. We'll just have to deal with it.'

Below them, inside the warehouse, Ann-li lay in the freezing dark. In the flickering light of the hurricane-lamp, Dooley performed his slow pull-ups on the beam. The mist hovered and swirled, but did not turn to fog, and through it came a flashing green light.

'Billy. Look.' From way downstream, there it was at

last: Potts's first signal. 'Told you it'd come. That means the Changs are all right, and Titch is on the way. Time for me to be off.' Sam got to his feet.

'Rather you than me,' said Billy grimly.

'Just stick to what we've talked about. By the time you get the *next* signal, I'll be in position. Right. Here we go!' Holding the rope, he crawled to the edge of the roof, eased over and looked back.

'Good luck, Billy.'

'You too.'

And then he was gone. The final and most dangerous stage of the rescue plan was under way.

9

THE RESCUE
OF ANN-LI

From the roof, Billy could hardly bear to watch as Sam slid quietly down the rope to the platform. He'd never been involved in a real adventure like this before, and now he was, he wasn't sure he liked it. It certainly wasn't quite what he'd imagined. The heroic headlines he had dreamed of seemed a very long way away.

Sam passed the door, then crouched to avoid being seen by Dooley as he slipped beneath the window. In no time he reached the ropes hanging down from the crane at the far corner of the platform. His aim was to get on to a narrow ledge that ran along the side of the warehouse, where he could wait, unobserved. He knew it wasn't going to be easy. Watching from above, Billy saw how far Sam would fall if he slipped, and the

124

strange swimming sensation in his head came back. He turned away, unable to look. He knew it would help if he occupied himself with something, so while Sam was endeavouring to get on to the ledge, he got on with the job of unfastening the rope from the derrick.

Sam's climb down had tightened the knot, but eventually Billy succeeded in loosening the sharp, rough fibres. He unthreaded the rope from the pulley and set off with it towards the far end of the roof at the back of the building. Here was part of a cast-iron staircase, the remains of an old fire escape, which Sam and Titch had spotted on their 'recce'. This was to be Billy's escape route. The problem was that it broke off halfway down, and didn't go anywhere. There was work to be done if Billy was to be able to use it successfully. He tested it with his foot. It was wobbly, but just firm enough to hold his weight. He inched his way down, one step at a time, until he reached the point where it ended. The side rails were rusting and unstable, so he knotted the rope to the lowest stair, and threw the long end into space. He didn't dare look down, but thought he heard it hit the ground. There was nothing else to be done for now. Unsteadily, he climbed back up.

Sam's hands were cold and sweaty with fear, and they

slipped a bit on the rope, but once he had crabbed his way to the corner of the building, he could use his knees to lever himself round on to the ledge along the side of the warehouse. It was not much wider than his foot, and it was difficult to get into a position he could hold indefinitely. It took him three or four goes before he was balanced firmly, clutching the rope. It was still precarious, but with his back to the wall and the rope in his hands, he was out of sight of the platform. In position, on the ledge, all he had to do was wait. He hoped it wouldn't be for too long.

Billy steeled himself and peeped over the edge of the roof, down on to the platform. He was pleased to see that Sam was not there – he must be ready – so he took some of the pebbles from his pocket and counted them into a row on the roof by the derrick. It was a mind game. When he was counting he didn't feel too queasy, but as soon as he remembered where he was he got panicky and his heart thumped high in his chest. He simply had to control himself and wait for the next signal. He looked downstream and uttered a quiet prayer: 'Come on, Titch. Please. Come on.'

Titch's boat was making steady progress, although the tide did make it hard going. But with Titch's easy, practised rowing rhythm, the prow was already nosing round the long curve in the river at Limehouse Reach. Titch was really keen to prove herself to Sam, and it was even more important to do so now that he knew she was a girl.

She could no longer see Potts on the bank. Looking the other way, she turned over her shoulder and saw the warehouse in the distance. The sight of the derelict building, looming ghostly out of the swathes of mist, brought home the real danger of what they were about to do. She heard Potts whistling through the dark. Looking over her shoulder towards the warehouse again, and judging that she was now near enough for Potts to give his second signal, Titch returned the whistle as agreed.

From the warehouse roof, Billy saw the green light flashing again. 'Phew! At last. Nice one, Potty!' he whispered to himself with relief. This signal meant that Titch was approaching, and Billy could move to the next stage of Sam's master plan. He picked up a handful of the pebbles, took a deep breath and lobbed them on to the platform below.

Balanced precariously on his ledge, Sam heard the pebbles hit the platform and tensed himself for action.

He listened and waited. Nothing happened. 'Hell,' he breathed. Suddenly one of his feet slipped and he lurched outwards from the building. He grabbed the rope tighter and battled to maintain his balance. Sweat formed instantly on his forehead, and stung his eyes. He flailed, and fought, and finally regained control. 'That was a bit close for comfort,' he said to himself. When his pulse-rate slowed down, he was able to concentrate and listen again. All was quiet. 'Come on, Billy. Come on. Try again.'

As if in answer to Sam's whispered plea, a second rainstorm of pebbles spattered on to the platform. This time, it had the intended effect. Almost immediately, Dooley burst out of the door. 'Who's there?' he demanded in his thick, guttural voice. As he came out further on to the platform, he trod on the pebbles. He stood a moment, trying to work out where they had come from. He kicked at them, and they scattered noisily over the metal platform. He looked up to the roof and called again, louder this time: 'Who's up there?'

In answer to his question, from the roof came a loud thudding noise. Billy was making good use of the big chunk of wood he had found.

'What the hell?' said Dooley. 'It's them bloody kids.'

Then he called out, 'If I get my hands on you lot, I'll wring your bleeding necks. D'you hear?'

'Nice one, Billy,' said Sam, grinning.

Inside the warehouse, the sound of Billy thumping the roof was like thunder, waking Ann-li with a start. She had given up her dream of being rescued, but when she heard the noise overhead, deep in her heart she began to hope again. Perhaps someone really was up there trying to help her.

As Sam had anticipated, Dooley could see that the chain from the derrick was the obvious way up on to the roof and he started to climb it. With ease, his great hands grasped the huge, oily links, as he hauled himself up arm over arm.

As soon as Billy saw the chain shifting, he knew that Dooley was climbing. He increased the speed of his drumming, and at the same time gradually moved closer to his getaway position above the staircase at the back of the roof. From this point on, they would have to move fast.

When Sam heard Billy drumming faster, he knew the moment was near when he must launch himself out on the rope and fly round on to the platform. He heard Billy yell – the sign that Dooley was nearing the top of the chain. Sam took a deep breath, gripped hard on the rope and shoved off with all his might. It all happened at lightning speed. As he swung round towards the platform, he looked up and saw Dooley near the roof. Suddenly, the platform was coming straight at him. He squeezed hard, balling himself up tight, and just made it, sliding on to the cold metal on his knees with hardly a sound. He let go of the rope, flattened himself against the wall and edged past the window. Just before Dooley climbed on to the roof he looked back down, but he was too late to see Sam nip into the warehouse through the open door.

Billy had not seen Dooley before, and the colossal size of the man that clambered over the ledge and stood upright on the roof in the moonlight sent a shiver down his spine. Billy was right by the top of the staircase – his escape route – keeping up a feverish drumming. Before Dooley had gathered himself, Billy threw the wood to distract him. 'Who's there?' Dooley asked again, moving towards the noise. Billy shot over the edge on to the rusty iron staircase. He was desperate to get away, and rushed down the flimsy, shaking stairs, trying not to think about the height. He got to the bottom step, knelt down, took hold of the rope and started to slide down it. For Billy, with his head swimming, it was a living nightmare. He began to slip down the rope so fast that his hands started to burn, but he managed to grip the rope with his feet and slow himself down. He could feel the end of the rope swaying wildly, and he realised with horror that it hadn't reached the ground. His feet suddenly found the end of it, and he clutched tighter with his hands and elbows, to bring himself to an agonizing halt. He didn't dare even open his eyes, so he dangled there, with no idea how far above the ground he was. At some point he would just have to let go. He couldn't imagine anything worse than floating through space, not knowing how far he had to fall, but he hadn't the strength left to think. He simply let go. The ground came up to meet him almost immediately. He expected to collapse in a heap, but found himself standing. He opened his eyes, and there, just above his outstretched hand, was the rope. He was on solid ground again. He doubled over with relief.

When he had recovered, he looked up to the roof, picked out against the pale moonlight. Up to that point his mind had been so full of just hanging on and surviving, he hadn't given much thought to Dooley, who – according to the plan – was supposed to follow Billy down the fire escape, but there was no sign of him. This was worrying. If Dooley went back down the chain from the derrick, he would most probably be back in the warehouse again before Sam had Ann-li out. Billy wanted to run away, but he was a conscientious lad, and he stopped himself. If Sam was going to have to deal with Dooley unexpectedly, Billy reckoned he might need help. So instead of saving his own skin, he began to work his way round to the quayside at the front of the warehouse. From there he might be able to see what was going on.

Dooley had found the fire escape pretty quickly, put his foot on it, and decided it wouldn't hold his weight. He scouted round, but could find no other way down, and reckoned he should get below again fast, to make sure Ann-li was still in her cell. He remembered only too clearly Maltravers's threats.

Sam had entered the warehouse with Titch's instructions clear in his mind. Dooley's hurricane-lamp cast some light, and by it he was able to find the door to Ann-li's room quite quickly – it was the only one that was bolted on the outside. He slid back the shutter and stared in. Ann-li was kneeling, still gagged and tethered, but waiting, hoping. Sam nipped inside, and whipped off her gag.

'Sam! How did you—?'

'We gotta be real quick, Ann-li. I'll explain when

you're out of here.' From his pocket he took a candle which he lit, and with his knife he began to cut through Ann-li's ropes. Feet first. Poor girl, trussed up like a turkey, he thought. When Ann-li's feet came free, she almost cried with pain as the blood flooded back into her freezing toes. She tried standing so that Sam could get at her hands more easily, but fell over; her muscles were weak from lack of use, and she would simply have to wait till the pins and needles wore off before she could move. Sam cut her hands free and then began rubbing Ann-li's feet for her.

'How's that? Can you walk?' She could. Just. With Sam's help. 'Come on, then, let's get moving.'

Sam blew the candle out, and with Ann-li's arm round his shoulder, he supported his friend out of the hateful room that had been her prison for so long.

Emerging from Ann-li's cell, they set off towards the door on to the platform. Suddenly, Sam stopped. 'Sssh. Listen.' He could hear noises from outside. 'Quick. This way.' He dragged Ann-li, half walking, half shuffling, towards the back of the warehouse, where they stumbled behind some old tea chests and threw themselves on the floor. Sam took a deep breath and peeped over. There, filling the doorway, in the pale misty moonlight, was

the massive silhouette of Dooley. Sam ducked down out of sight. 'Bloody 'ell, Ann-li,' he whispered. 'We're trapped.'

10

THE GREAT DETECTIVE

Dooley hovered in the warehouse doorway, checking outside before moving in. He couldn't see anything obviously wrong, and he didn't quite understand what was going on, but he was on edge – baffled and angry. He collected the hurricane-lamp from his room and strode towards Ann-li's cell. When he found the door unbolted, he stood numb with disbelief – he didn't even have to look inside to know that Ann-li was no longer there. He rested his head on the door jamb and just said, 'No-ooo.' Sam and Ann-li watched. What would he do now?

When Billy reached the quayside, he stared up at the platform. He was hoping, listening for some sign of

Sam or Ann-li. He was so intent on the ladder and the platform high above, that he didn't sense there was another person in the dark with him. He was an innocent. He was not streetwise. He heard nothing, he knew nothing, until a hand, strong as iron, went round his mouth and silenced him. Another hand held him firm, and pinned him to the wall. The strength of his attacker was overwhelming. Billy kicked out, but to no effect. It must be that horrible, evil Colonel, he thought to himself in panic. He tried to yell out, and to bite the hand clamped firmly over his mouth, but he didn't stand a chance against the fierce strength of his assailant. When he finally caught a glimpse of the man who had him at his mercy, he was amazed. It was the filthy old tramp, the old dosser, who was hissing at him, 'Ssshhh. Be quiet.' Again, Billy tried to kick and bite him – there was nothing else he could do.

'Ssshhh. Not a sound, my boy.'

The old dosser's voice took him by surprise – it was clean and cultivated, quite at odds with the dirty, ragged appearance of the man. Billy recognised it. But who was it? Then, to his amazement, he heard his name. 'Billy . . .' The old dosser shook him. 'Billy . . . for heaven's sake, boy, what's the matter with you?' In a flash, Billy realised who it was . . .

'Mr Holmes!' It was a miracle! Billy stopped struggling and turned to look at his hero. 'It's you, Mr Holmes!'

'At last!' Before Billy had time to collect himself the Great Detective turned him towards the ladder. 'Follow me, Billy, my boy. Quick now! You can swim, can't you, Billy?'

'Yes, Mr Holmes, sir.'

'Good. Don't get behind, boy. We must move fast.'

With Holmes taking the lead, they began to climb.

Edie's sisters took it in turns to look after her. They had to share the same bed anyway. Her frail body was rigid with tension. She kept murmuring, 'Fall. Falling. Water.' None of them had any idea what she was talking about, they just had to wait patiently for her to come through. Dr Watson had assured them that she would.

Ann-li's feet and legs came slowly back to life as she and Sam watched Dooley, who was considering where he should begin his search: the other rooms like the one where Ann-li had been held? The wooden pallets strewn along the side of the warehouse, by the gallery? Or the tea chests, where Sam and Ann-li were hiding?

With uncanny instinct, Dooley headed straight for the tea chests. Sam and Ann-li ducked down.

Dooley got closer and closer. Crouched down low, peeping between the chests, Sam and Ann-li saw him loom larger and more threatening than ever, the flickering light from the hurricane-lamp glinting on his scarred cheek. They could hear him talking to himself, low and guttural: 'If I find them, I'll wring their bleeding necks.' They could hear his heavy breathing.

'I'll see if I can distract him,' whispered Sam. 'Just see if you can get out. Don't worry about me. Ready?'

He was on the point of breaking out when a knock came from the door on to the platform, which Dooley had not closed. Dooley stopped, confused. Then, from behind him, came a loud call: 'Mr Dooley.'

Dooley turned. 'Eh?'

The door at the far end of the warehouse opened a little more, and again Dooley heard his name. Sam and Ann-li watched with baited breath. As the door opened fully, they were astonished to see the old dosser.

'What the hell?' said Dooley. Furious, he moved swiftly towards the intruding beggar. 'Get out, you. Get out!' He now had his back to Sam and Ann-li.

'Let's go for it, Ann-li,' urged Sam. With Dooley distracted, they ran towards the door, aiming to use the cover of the wooden pallets ranged along the side by the gallery railings.

Dooley approached the old dosser, who asked, with cheeky civility, 'I was wondering, Mr Dooley, sir, if you might spare me the cost of a cup o' tea.'

Dooley put the lamp on the floor, grabbed the tramp and steered him back to the door.

'Get out, you stinking layabout. What the devil do you think you're doing up here?'

He had no idea of course that he was grappling hand to hand with Sherlock Holmes himself. Holmes, for his part, was well aware that Sam and Ann-li – making their getaway – had now made the safety of the pallets and were working their way behind them towards the door. Holmes's aim was simply to distract Dooley long enough for them to get out. Protesting, he allowed Dooley to force him backwards towards the door.

'I was only asking the price of a pint o' tea, Mr Dooley!'

Dooley was pushing the old dosser out on to the platform, and at this bit of cheek, he gave him a hard shove in the chest.

'Get your filthy hands off me, you dog!' cried the old dosser – Billy, watching from the platform, was astonished by Holmes's performance – 'Who d'you

think I am, you great bruiser? I got me dignity.'

As the two grappling figures emerged on to the platform, Billy yelled at Dooley, 'You leave him alone, you big bully.'

Dooley still had the old dosser by the collar, but with Billy yelling at him, and Holmes muttering, 'Sorry, mate. Sorry. Forget it. Forget it,' his attention was successfully diverted from his search for Ann-li.

Dooley threw the old dosser aside, lunging viciously across the platform at Billy. For such a large man, he was deceptively fast in his movement, but Billy ducked and ran towards the warehouse door. Suddenly, he could see Sam and Ann-li coming fast towards him, and realised that he had to lure Dooley in the opposite direction, so they could get out. Swiftly he darted round Holmes. Dooley stumbled as he too tried to get past the old dosser, who cunningly blocked his path. Dooley chased Billy to the corner of the platform by the ropes from the crane. The idea crossed Billy's mind fleetingly that he could nip *down* the ropes, but Dooley was too quick for him and Billy found himself cornered, backing towards the front edge of the platform that overhung the river. Holmes lunged and grabbed Dooley by the leg, but Dooley shook him off, and advanced on Billy, who could now see the river fifty feet below. His head began to swim again. Dooley's enormous hands were almost on him. He wavered for a moment, but Dooley was so close he had no option – he plucked up all his courage, dipped under Dooley's reaching arm, and with a colossal yell, leaped into the darkness. In lunging and missing, Dooley fell face down, right on the edge of the platform. He lay there cursing, and watching as Billy plummeted downwards, landing with a great splash in the freezing river.

Edie's scream woke the whole family. She began to flail and struggle in her fever, fighting for breath. 'Don't drown. Don't drown,' she shouted. Her father tried to restrain her, but she appeared to panic, and was best left alone. There was nothing anyone could do. They simply sat and watched as she fought whatever demon it was that she was wrestling with. In spite of Watson's words of comfort, they began to fear that they would lose her.

When Billy hit the water, the shock of the cold, and the force of the blow, hit him hard. He went down and down. In his stunned imagination it seemed that he would never stop. He could feel the grip of the tide, and strove to keep the icy water out of his lungs. He took a mouthful – filthy and freezing – and began to panic. He was desperate to breathe. He struggled to swim upwards, and at last, his head broke the surface. He thrashed about in the choppy water, trying to recover himself. At last, he managed to take in some air, and his lungs began to clear. Then he became aware of a strange noise nearby: 'Psssst.'

'What?' he gasped, flailing round to see where the sound came from.

'Psssst – over 'ere.'

He rubbed the water from his eyes, and there, under the platform, at the foot of the ladder, in the boat, he could see Titch. He was so relieved that he struck out hard, and within seconds, Titch was hauling him aboard.

'Boy!' said Billy. 'Am I glad to see you!'

'You, too,' said Titch. 'Nice of you to drop by.'

Up on the platform, Dooley was getting to his feet as Sam and Ann-li charged out through the door and went straight for the trapdoor, left open for them by Holmes. Dooley moved fast to prevent them, but was blocked by Holmes, who ran hard and low, head-butting him in the belly. With Dooley temporarily laid out, Holmes was able to shut the trapdoor, giving Sam and Ann-li a better chance of making their getaway down the ladder. As the trapdoor slammed shut, Dooley fell on the old tramp, striking out viciously. He was surprised by his strength and skill. Dooley, of course, was still not aware that the old dosser was Sherlock Holmes himself, nor that Holmes was an expert in martial arts. Dooley was stronger, but Holmes was more agile and much cleverer.

As Sam and Ann-li sped down the ladder, below them Billy and Titch were yelling, 'Come on! Come on! We're here! Come on!' The fleeing pair slid down the last few rungs and leaped into the boat. Ann-li went to the prow; Billy, wrapped in one of the rugs, pushed off from the side. With Sam on one oar, Titch on the other, and the tide in their favour, they struck out.

'Who was that old tramp?' asked Ann-li.

'What tramp?' enquired Titch, setting a good rowing rhythm.

'That old tramp who helped us out just now,' said Ann-li.

'It was that old dosser from The Chief, Titch,' said Sam, following Titch's lead and pulling strongly on his oar. 'He turned up in the nick of time. Bit odd, but it saved our bacon!'

'That was no old dosser,' said Billy proudly. 'I know exactly who that was.' They all looked at him in disbelief. 'I tell you – *that* . . . was Mr Sherlock Holmes.'

'What?!' Titch couldn't believe her ears.

'The Great Detective?' said Ann-li – even she had heard of Sherlock Holmes.

There was an air of stunned amazement in the little boat.

'Sherlock Holmes?' said Titch, rowing lustily. 'Stone me!'

'Yeah,' said Billy smugly. 'He's a master of disguise.'

'You see, Billy me ol' pal?' said Sam. 'I told you we'd locate him, didn't I?'

Turning to his fellow oarsman, Sam smiled. Titch returned his grin and the two of them struck out harder than ever.

Looking back up at the platform, they could see Dooley and Holmes silhouetted against the moon, locked in deadly combat. Fused together in their struggle, they looked like some strange creature, one man with two heads, writhing and swaying on the platform. Suddenly Holmes broke free. He was about to deliver a crushing punch to Dooley's jaw, when Dooley – determined to try and recapture the escaping hostage – dived.

From the boat, they gaped in awe at the perfect arc of Dooley's flight. In spite of his immense size, there was little splash as he entered the water. Within seconds he was up and swimming. He had an almost lazy style that drove him through the water at a deceptive pace, narrowing the gap between swimmer and boat. Sam and Titch increased their rowing rate, but Dooley – swimming in the calmer slipstream of the boat – was gaining on them.

'Billy! The stones!' panted Sam.

'They're down there!' yelled Titch.

Billy felt around on the floor of the boat and found the bag of stones that Potts had left. By now, Dooley was within striking distance; soon his pounding arms would be able to stretch out and grab the stern. Billy tossed the bag to Ann-li. He still had some for himself, left over in his pocket. Together they began to pelt Dooley.

So that's what the stones were for, thought Titch, impressed again with Sam's planning and forethought. The stones hit the water round Dooley's head like bullets. Bombarded and winded, he began to lose his rhythm, and the boat started to pull away from him. He laboured on, losing ground, until suddenly, with a furious yell of frustration, he gave up, hitting the water in anger. A great cheer came from the little boat.

From high above on the platform, Sherlock Holmes was able to see the small boat and its plucky crew making their getaway in the misty moonlight. He saw them defeat Dooley. He heard their cheer. He was pleased for them, but if Maltravers was to be arrested, and Moriarty's organisation dented, if any real good were to come of this dark episode, there was work to be done. He must get out of his disguise and make contact with Watson and Lestrade as fast as possible. There was not a moment to lose.

The little boat made steady progress down river – helped now by the current. They had Ann-li on board. They had escaped Dooley. They were heading for safety. Now, there was only one stage of Sam's plan left to go.

11

MORNING

Ann-li's family was safe aboard the Captain's wherry, waiting. Potts was above, keeping watch for Titch and the rescue boat. The Captain had agreed to look after the Chang family during the rescue, and Sam had persuaded him to take them all with him when he sailed at midnight on the full tide. This was the final masterstroke of Sam's plan. The Captain would take the Changs to the north-east coast near the borders with Scotland, where they would be able to start a new life somewhere remote, far from the clutches of Maltravers and the vengeful Dragon clan. Ann-li's father, mother, baby brother and Uncle Fu were all there, huddled together in the warmth of the Captain's cabin, waiting and hoping for the return of their beloved Ann-li.

'They're here!' Potts's triumphant yell brought the Changs out on deck. The small craft came into view, emerging through the light mist, like a mirage. As the little rowing-boat drew nearer, they saw with joy that Ann-li was on board. Willing hands helped the little band of heroes down into the cosy cabin – it was a welcome relief after their night of cold and danger. Ann-li was crying, clinging to her mother. Billy was able to dry off. Potts just beamed. Titch led the applause for Sam.

In spite of the atmosphere of jubilation, Sam was depressed; he felt he had failed. Had it not been for the intervention of the old dosser – Holmes – the rescue attempt might not have been successful. Needing to be alone, he went on deck, and watched as the Captain tied his rowing-boat – the rescue boat – to the wherry and hung out the green lamp that Potts had used to signal on the starboard bow.

'Thanks, Captain. We couldn't have done it without you.'

'Glad to be of 'elp, m'lad. Won't be long before we're orf now. You can tell them I be nearly ready.'

Sam stuck his head into the cabin. 'It'll soon be time.'

Chang drew him inside. 'Sam, I don't know how to thank you.'

'I'm sorry you've got to go, Mr Chang,' said Sam. 'I'll miss you all. You're like family to me.'

'Colonel Maltravers will not be pleased.'

'You could say that.'

'You must understand, Sam. This man Maltravers is evil . . . but it is not just him . . .' Again his hand strayed to the faded dragon tattoo on his forearm. 'Do you understand me?' Sam nodded. 'Be careful, Sam.'

'I will, sir. Good luck.'

'Time to go,' called the Captain. He was ready to depart.

Ann-li, with her arms round her dad, said, 'Bye, Sam. Thanks. Thanks a lot.'

'It was all of us.'

'Yes, of course – my thanks to all of you.' Ann-li shook all their hands. 'I hardly know your names, and you risked so much for me. Billy. Titch. Potts? And you, Sam, my friend. Thank you all.'

The band of four made their goodbyes, wished the Changs well, and jumped ashore. Potts was rubbing Billy's arms to keep him warm. Titch untied the mooring-ropes, and quietly, the wherry eased away. The Captain waved. As the wherry grew smaller Sam slipped further into gloom.

Titch came and stood by Sam, watching. On the departing wherry, they could still see the Changs clinging to each other – a family reunited – something neither of them had now. Titch looked at Sam. She wondered why he seemed depressed when things had ended so well.

'You seem down, Sam.'

'I am, Titch. I envy them.'

'Me too,' said Titch. Sharing this sense of envy made them feel close to each other, and vulnerable. 'But . . . Sam . . .'

'But what?'

Titch was unable to reply, and felt self-conscious.

'What?' repeated Sam.

'Doesn't matter.'

'I know what you're thinking, Titch.'

'Do you?'

'Reckon.'

'It's just that . . . what I'm trying to say, Sam, is . . . I really . . . like . . .' Titch faltered. She wanted to say she felt at home with Sam. That she liked his kindness to her. That she liked *him*. If Sam hadn't rumbled her secret, it would have been easier – as a boy she could just have said it – but Titch couldn't finish her sentence. What she didn't realise was that Sam

153

didn't need to be told. He understood.

'Don't say it, Titch. You don't have to. If you say it, you'll mess it up.'

So they stood together in silence and watched until they could no longer see the Changs and the distant wherry. Until Potts joined them, and brought them down to earth.

'Come on, you two. Time to go 'ome. It's only just up the road for you, but me and Billy 'ave got quite an 'ike! You don't 'appen to 'ave the cost of the cab-fare, do you?'

Next morning just before dawn, Maltravers, white with fury, made his way to Chang's Seamen's Hostel followed by a sour-looking Dooley. Ann-li may have got away, but he intended to relieve his anger by punishing her father. To their surprise, the hostel doors were unlocked. The beds on which the smokers usually lay were unoccupied, the pipes unlit. The place was deserted. Maltravers rounded on Dooley.

'This is your fault, you halfwit.'

'I don't see—'

'Look upstairs.'

Obediently, Dooley left the room. Maltravers, the wicked smile finally wiped from his lips, was contemplating his revenge, when from above he heard a cry from Dooley, followed by the sounds of a scuffle. Maltravers was moving towards the stairway, when Dooley called again.

'They've got me, Colonel!'

The thought of helping Dooley never occurred to Maltravers – the man's fate was of no concern to him. He turned, and without hesitation, shot out of the front door of the hostel. He found his way blocked by four very large policemen. And Inspector Lestrade. Maltravers glared at them in silent contempt.

'Perhaps you would like to go back inside, Colonel Maltravers. There is someone who wishes to meet you,' said Lestrade.

Maltravers turned, wordless, but before he could re-enter the hostel, he found himself face to face with Sherlock Holmes. His reptilian eyes narrowed. His neck straightened. He looked more than ever like a snake preparing to strike. Holmes merely smiled.

'So, Colonel. What a pleasure it is to meet you. Particularly under these circumstances.'

'Mr Holmes,' hissed Maltravers, with icy assurance, 'I shall have my revenge. On you. And on those interfering children.'

'We shall see, Colonel, we shall see. Inspector

Lestrade, I think it is time for you to take the Colonel and Mr Dooley to the comfort of Scotland Yard.'

Dawn was breaking, dispersing the light mist, as Maltravers and Dooley were led away, down to the dockside. The only sound to violate the silence was the shuffle of boots on cobblestones, the chink of handcuffs, and the suck and swirl of the river.

In the McArdle home – the crowded little nest in the 'rookeries' of Lisson Grove – Edie's fever had subsided. She was calm. She looked peaceful and untroubled. She no longer murmured. Watson had been right. She was well again, and her family was tired but grateful.

The Chang family, on board the Captain's wherry, was sailing towards the freedom of the sea, and beyond that, to their new life. As they left the mouth of the River Thames, they headed north. Far away over the horizon to their right, the sun broke dazzling and warm.

12

TEA, TOAST AND . . .

'**P**otts! Elbows off the table!'

'Beg your p, Mrs H.'

Mrs Hudson's kitchen was unusually crowded. Billy, in his page-boy uniform, sat at the head of the table like the cock of the walk. Potts, in his smartest waistcoat, was taking care of Edie, dressed in her Sunday best, green ribbons in her hair.

'Anuvver cuppa, Edie?'

'Yes please, Potts.' Edie showed not a trace of her feverish night, and was thoroughly enjoying being spoiled by Potts, who was in fine form.

'Dandy cuppa cha, Mrs H.'

Sam and Titch, washed and brushed up, felt a little out of place in the unfamiliar atmosphere of a family tea. Mrs Hudson's kitchen was homely, but it was grander than anything either of them had ever seen. They were enjoying themselves, but they were quiet.

Their host, Sherlock Holmes, had listened intently to his guests for some half an hour as they recounted their part in the rescue of Ann-li, and then he excused himself. His mind was full of Moriarty, and he also recognised that his presence might well limit their enjoyment. As soon as the Great Detective had gone up to his study, the children attacked the lavish spread prepared by Mrs Hudson.

'You know wot, Mrs H?' quipped Potts. Mrs Hudson's eyes narrowed. 'You ought to put this raspberry jam of yours on the market! And this 'oney! If me 'n' Edie sold "Mrs 'Udson's 'ome-made 'oney", as well as 'erbs, you'd make a flippin' fortune. And we'd only take twenty per cent commission, wouldn't we, Edie?'

'Sure, he's a fine salesman, Mrs Hudson,' said Edie.

'I'm not sure Mr Holmes would approve,' replied Mrs Hudson, unsmiling.

''E'd never know,' said Potts.

'I wouldn't bank on it. He don't miss a trick,' said Sam.

Titch shifted uncomfortably.

'Master Wiggins is right,' said Mrs Hudson firmly.

'Come on, now, all of you. Eat up. Dr Watson will be back soon!'

'Dr Watson?!' said Potts. 'Listen . . . I got an idea . . .'

Watson had left early for work, and had been out all day. After a morning of house visits, he had treated himself to lunch in Kensington and attended a lecture at the Science Museum. The remainder of his afternoon had been taken up with the crush of patients at his Paddington surgery.

Returning home, still ignorant of events leading to the arrest of Maltravers and Dooley, his Gladstone bag seemed heavier than usual. He was gloomily hanging his coat and hat in the hall, when he caught sight of Mrs Hudson by her kitchen door.

'Still no sign of Mr Holmes, I suppose?'

'No, Doctor. None,' said Mrs Hudson, po-faced. Watson was too depressed to hear the sounds of stifled giggling from inside the kitchen. 'Excuse me, Doctor, I have something on the stove.' Mrs Hudson turned into her kitchen, wagged a finger at Potts, and put it to her lips to shush him.

It was Potts's idea of course, to play this trick on Watson. As the weary Doctor plodded up the stairs, he fancied once again that he could hear the strains of Holmes's violin. He paused. The rich, dark melancholy of the tune was more than fancy. 'Holmes!?!' he cried in disbelief, bounding up the last few stairs and bursting into the study.

Holmes, in his long dressing-gown, was seated on a large cushion by the fire, which provided the only light in the room. Its ruddy glow gave the scene a Hell-like appearance. Ignoring Watson, who stood amazed in the doorway, Holmes continued to play. Suddenly he stopped.

'Where have you been, Watson?'

'Where have *I* been, Holmes?' Holmes turned to the fire, and Watson caught sight of his face: his fine high brow was creased with pain, his eyes glowered with suffering. 'Holmes! What on earth is wrong?'

'You would not understand, my dear Watson.'

'I do not expect ever to understand you, my dear friend, but I think you owe me, at the very least, an explanation. I have been at my wits' end, worrying about you.'

'Forgive me, Watson. Secrecy was essential. And now, I am weighed down by the blackest of thoughts.'

'Moriarty?' Holmes nodded. 'I knew it.'

'I cannot abide explanations, but you are right, I *do*

owe you one.' He placed his violin to one side.

He told Watson the whole story of Chang's past, of the Dragons, and the kidnap of Ann-li, concluding, 'However, I have had a remarkable experience, Watson. I have had the privilege of observing a small group of young people taking great risks – ah, youth, there is nothing like it. Individually these street urchins are interesting. As a team, they are astonishing! Their leader, one Wiggins, is quite exceptional. I wonder if you will remember the boy; we bumped into him once. Or to be more precise, he bumped into us.'

'How extraordinary!' exclaimed Watson.

Holmes talked of Sam's skills in planning, of Potts – a heart of gold concealed beneath a joky exterior – and of Billy – who had shown a bravery of which Holmes had not thought him capable. Edie's powers fascinated him. Titch had kept away from him, and Holmes was pretty sure that he knew why!

'These children, Watson, have pitted themselves against two bad men in the name of – what? Friendship? Loyalty? Heroism even, one might go so far. Only Wiggins is aware that wider forces are at work.' Watson nodded. 'If the truth be told, they may have hindered me. Yesterday – the night of the rescue – Maltravers had a meeting with Moriarty where I

might have apprehended him, had I not been concerned about these children's safety.' He sighed. 'But I envy them now. They are happily eating their tea with Mrs Hudson . . .'

'Yes, I thought there was something going on.'

'. . . For a moment they can forget what a vile world we live in.'

'The world is not to blame, Holmes, for what we make of it.'

'It is a vile world, Watson, a vile world . . . in which the blessings of home and health are denied to the poor, *because* they are poor.'

'It is pointless arguing with you, Holmes. I shall go and see Billy, and meet these children.'

'Promise me that their exploits will not be chronicled in the same vulgar way that you present my own inadequacies to the reading public.'

'I shall pretend I didn't hear that last remark of yours, Holmes.'

'I am quite serious, Watson – once their existence is made public, their lives are at risk.'

His tail between his legs, Watson departed.

After the strain of his conversation with Holmes, Watson found the atmosphere in the kitchen a positive tonic. To be sure, the boisterousness diminished a little with the Doctor's entrance, but Watson observed even Mrs Hudson's rare good humour! Once they had enjoyed the joke they had played at Watson's expense, Potts, urged on by Billy, was telling outrageous stories of Jacky Dyke, his notorious boss.

'Go on, Potts. Tell the one about the giant cucumber!'

'I'm not sure that'd be quite suitable for Mrs H's delicate ears, Billy!'

Watson sat and listened. When Potts's supply of anecdotes dried up, he talked with the children. He liked the company of young people, and because of his somewhat bluff manner, and a genuine naivety of spirit, they liked him. He was pleased to meet Sam again, under happier circumstances than two years before. Sam was shy with him, but encouraged by the others, he recounted his side of the story, and when he was done, it was with genuine admiration that Watson remarked, 'To think that Lestrade and I were at a loss, while you children . . . well, I am astonished. Impressed.'

The thought struck him that the children's lives would seem dull to them now that this exciting episode was concluded. Suddenly, Holmes burst into the kitchen.

'WATSON!' he cried, pulling up a chair and sitting at the table. He spoke to Watson with great urgency, in hushed, confidential tones. Watson could see that he was in the grip of some new and sudden inspiration.

'Why did I not think of it before, Watson? It has been staring me in the face, and I have not seen it. These urchins can be of more use to me than dozens of the regular force.'

'You cannot use them instead of policemen, Holmes!'

'Why on earth not? The mere sight of an official-looking person seals men's lips, but these youngsters go everywhere, see everything, and overhear everyone.' He spoke as if the 'youngsters' to whom he referred were not in the room.

'Holmes. Their lives are not yours to use and command.'

'I shall give them something to live for . . .'

'You will place them in great danger.'

''Old on, Doc!' Who but Potts would dare to interrupt such a conversation? 'Mr 'Olmes is on to somefin' 'ere. If we get ourselves organised, we're the perfect team – ain't we? We got Sam, who's a finker, and Titch, who can climb anyfink and get in anywhere.

Billy's got the courage of ⸺ꭃᴜ. Edie's the perfect mole – she can 'ear a leaf move a 'undred yards away. And me – I'm in charge of the business side. Should you wish to talk about fees, Mr Dyke don't usually require my services before lunch, an' I can be available most mornings.'

There was an amused silence in the kitchen. All eyes turned to Sherlock Holmes.

'Well, Watson? I rest my case.'

'But, Holmes, if Moriarty is to be feared . . .'

'Indeed he is!'

'. . . all the more reason *not* to involve these children,' cried Watson.

'All the more reason for them to join in the fight for a just world – it will soon be *their* world after all!' Holmes was adamant, his tone final.

Watson looked round the table for support, but the only sympathetic face was Mrs Hudson's, and she did not speak; wisely, she kept out of Holmes's affairs.

'Well, Holmes,' said Watson grudgingly, 'I can see your mind is set, and there is nothing anyone can say that will change it.'

'Correct, Watson!'

'I do not approve at all of what you are suggesting, Holmes. It is downright irregular.'

Holmes regarded his disgruntled friend, his face wreathed in smiles.

'My dear Watson, you are a genius.'

'What? What on earth are you talking about?'

'Did you not say "irregular", Watson?'

'You know I did, Holmes. And I jolly well meant it. Using children as unofficial policemen is *most* irregular.'

'Then that, my dear Watson, is what we shall call them: *the* Irregulars! The *Baker Street* Irregulars. Sherlock Holmes's Irregulars!'

For a moment it looked as though Holmes would have the last word, but then Holmes didn't often come up against characters like Potts!

'Dr W, I would just like to make it clear that the fact that you come up wiv our name – the Irregulars – will, of course, be given due financial consideration. That's elementary!'

Even Holmes laughed. Poor Watson was speechless.

'Sorry, Doc . . .' grinned Potts, 'game, set and match to the Great Detective!'

Sam and Titch were the last to leave Baker Street. They felt they were being drawn into something outside their understanding, and this made them uneasy. They had to fight hard to keep charge of their difficult lives, and they didn't like the idea of relinquishing the smallest bit of control. As they reached the front door, they were waylaid by Dr Watson.

'Well, Sam, how extraordinary that our paths should cross again in this way. I remember you so clearly from that night. Do you remember meeting me?'

'I do, sir. You was very kind to me. You gave me . . . some money.'

'Did I now?' exclaimed Watson. 'I don't remember that.'

'Well, you did, sir. I shall never forget it. You gave me two pennies.'

'A small enough gift. I trust it proved to be of assistance.'

'It did, sir,' said Sam. 'It turned my life around. You told me to start saving. And I have, ever since.'

'Good for you, Sam, good for you.' Then after a moment's thought: 'What is going to happen to you, now, I wonder, now that Mr Holmes has these plans for you?'

Sam was quiet.

'I'm not against 'elping,' said Titch, 'I just don't understand what *we're* gonna get out of it.'

'Indeed, young man. That is just one of my many concerns.'

168

Both Titch and Sam noticed with pleasure that Watson addressed Titch as 'young man'.

'Well, perhaps we could talk about it, sir,' said Sam, 'cos I've got an idea about what it might mean.'

'Have you, Sam? Good. What a remarkable boy you are. Well, we *shall* talk about it, and I can assure you that I will do whatever I can to assist you.'

Sam was thinking how nice it would be to sleep under the table in Mrs Hudson's warm kitchen, instead of under the bar at The Chief, but it seemed that Watson had other ideas.

'Might I perhaps offer you a little further financial assistance?'

'We did it for our friend, we didn't do it for money!' Sam protested.

'I wasn't suggesting you did,' said Watson. 'I was just offering you some additional help, until we have time for our talk, that's all.'

'It feels funny taking money now, sir. Though we're always short.'

'Well, I would very much like to give you both a little something, and I will expect you for our talk this Saturday afternoon – would five o'clock suit? Will you both come?'

Sam looked at Titch, who nodded.

Sam put out his hand. 'Thank you, sir. It's a deal.'

'A deal? Good,' said Watson, taking Sam's hand and shaking it firmly. He gave them two threepenny bits each. They protested. He insisted. 'Spend one, and save the other . . .'

'As your dear mother used to say,' said Sam.

'Indeed she did. What a memory you have. Until Saturday, then. Goodbye.'

'Goodbye, sir. And thank you.'

When tea was over and the kitchen was her own again, Mrs Hudson was able to restore calm. She invited Billy to sit by the fire with her, so he could tell her more about his part in the amazing adventure. He could hardly believe that he had been involved in a real crime, and that he had really helped to foil Maltravers and Dooley – he had conveniently forgotten that his original intention had been to find Holmes! But Mrs H did not want to take away from his achievements, and happily served him an extra cup of tea as she tidied and quizzed him about Ann-li's rescue. She was amazed that this chubby little dreamer who was always getting under her feet was capable of such daring. What had that cheeky young Potts said. Billy had the courage of a lion? Well . . . she would never see him in the same light again.

Potts took Edie home, and this time Edie persuaded him to come in. Her sisters and mother were all still out at work, but Edie's dad was there. Potts could easily see where Edie got her red hair and Irish brogue from! Her dad welcomed Potts warmly to their humble, cramped home – not much more than one room. When they were seated, he told Potts about his job as a salesman with the telephone company – he certainly had the gift of the gab – and explained to Potts how the telephone worked. Potts was interested, but still firmly convinced that it was newfangled nonsense.

'Newfangled?' cried Edie's dad in disbelief. 'I'm tellin' ya, Potty me lad, the first Telephone Company Directory has been available to subscribers for over ten years! I tell you that before the turn of the century, we shall be able to talk directly to people in America.'

'Pull the uvver one, Mr McArdle!'

'No. It's my prediction that there will be a cable all the way under the Atlantic. Take me word for it! They're working on it now! It'll happen, I'm tellin' ya! And I want a piece of the action.'

'But what about drinking water, Pop?' Edie piped up. 'That's Potts's idea. And let's face it, it would be nice, wouldn't it – water you could trust?'

'Ah! But the money is to be made through

mass consumption, Edie my beauty. You gotta sell in numbers.'

'But that's what's wrong wiv the telephone, Mr Mac. It's expensive, ennit? The fing wiv water is, we all need it. It's got to be a winner.'

Mr McArdle paused for a moment and nodded.

'He's right you know, Pop.'

'Well, I tell you what, young fella me lad,' said Mr McArdle, turning to Potts, 'I'll speak to a friend of mine about it, and get back to ya. Anyway, that's more than enough of me and the telephone, what have you two been up to? And you all dressed up, Edie!'

'It'd take too long to tell, Pop.'

'Well, at least you're up and about again. She had a bad night, my little daughter, you know,' he said, stroking Edie's hair and adjusting her ribbons. 'We thought she was a goner at one point. And we don't want that, do we?'

'We most certainly don't, Mr Mac,' said Potts vigorously.

'I think you've a soft spot for my Edie, don't you, Potts?'

Potts blushed, and for once was lost for words.

'Leave it out, Pop,' said Edie.

'What *happened* last night?' asked Potts.

'She can tell ya herself. I'll leave you two alone.' Mr McArdle gave Edie a peck on the cheek. 'I must get out for me evening shift.' And he went off to work.

'Are you all right now then, Edie?' asked Potts, worried.

'Sure, I am. I just had a bad night of seeing things, that's all. Worst ever – it's because I was worried about you.'

'You weren't, were you?'

'Sure I was – boats, rivers, dragons – you know, all that stuff you took the mickey out of.'

'But I had the easiest time of the lot. It was Billy who really done the biz! I mean he was right there in the fick of it! An' I tell you wot, Edie, I'll never not believe anyfink you say, ever again!'

'Ah, you say that now, Potts, but when Mr Holmes gets you working, sure, you won't be listening to me now, will you?'

'Ah, but I will, Edie.'

'Promise?'

'I promise. I promise.'

'Well, Potts, I shall hold you to that,' said Edie. And she held her hand out, hoping that Potts would take it. And to her pleasure and surprise, he did.

* * *

As Potts and Edie sat holding hands, Sam and Titch were making the long trek back to the Isle of Dogs. They had money in their hands, and though they felt empty now their adventure was over, they had each other.

EPILOGUE

DR WATSON'S DIARY
– AN UNPUBLISHED
FRAGMENT

DR WATSON

Holmes and I frequently have disagreements, but this evening we had a major dispute. The subject was these children – whom he insists on referring to as the Baker Street Irregulars – as though they were some sort of unofficial branch of the regular police force. He is determined to use them in his fight against crime, and most worrying of all, he feels that they can be of real use in his personal crusade against Moriarty. When in the grip of his obsessions he displays an inhumanity which dumbfounds me. What to do?

1. If I were to publish the facts about these children – against Holmes's will – it might prevent him using them in a way of which I so strenuously disapprove.
2. On the other hand, if I reveal *their* identities, Holmes will simply find other children. The moment they outlive their usefulness, he will do this anyway.
3. They are young teenage children, so as they grow older, their use will be short-lived.
4. Rather than fighting Holmes openly, I might combat him by ensuring they are taken care of secretly – making it my private mission, as it were, to look after them.

The results of some research . . .

EDIE MCARDLE

Edie McArdle. She has unusual gifts, gifts that, as a man of science, I find it hard to understand. But I now have clear evidence of her extrasensory skills that is difficult to ignore. I intend to begin a case-study of these experiences. Holmes is of the view that such powers, correctly harnessed, could be used to great effect. We both, therefore, wish to use her, for different reasons. I must ensure that she is protected. I can do most for her by helping her retain her eyesight for as long as possible.

BILLY CHIZZELL

Billy Chizzell. Billy and I have never really got on that well. He's a rather pushy young fellow who thinks I am a stupid old duffer. Well, it doesn't hurt me for him to think so. The only time he is ever relaxed with me is when we talk about Edie – he knows I am no duffer when it comes to medicine. He has the benefits, as she does, of a good family. His father would be happy if Billy followed him into regular work as a railway porter, but it is evident that his mother has rather grander aspirations. She sees him as the manager of a small bed and breakfast establishment close to the station, and is pushing him (he is her only child) hard in that direction. I'm not sure he has the brains to create or manage such a venture. That said, he displayed unexpected courage in the kidnap rescue. I must endeavour to overcome my lack of sympathy for him. I will make enquiries of an old army friend of mine, as to how a young man might gain entry to, or at any rate experience in, the world of hotel management.

POTTS

Potts (Eli). Well, Potts is a caution. Gets it from his mother. Returning from a visit to the Royal Academy, I ventured into Soho to find the pub in which she works — The Silken Garter if you will! On Berwick Street. Surprisingly pleasant. Full of locals with a deal of most amusing chatter. Leila Potts — everyone calls her Lily – is the life and soul of the place. Being the good Jewish mother she is, she believes that with the right experience Potts could run his own shop. She fancies the grocery trade. She is rather concerned that he does not become more involved in the world of betting, and discourages Potts's connection with Jacky Dyke, although young Eli has certainly learned a few things about salesmanship from that colourful gentleman. Potts's father came into the pub whilst I was there. A policeman! Accompanied by one or two rather unsavoury friends. Not at all the right company for one of the 'Regulars'!

SAM WIGGINS

The boy Wiggins (Sam). Prior to my meeting with him, and assisted by Billy – already we are getting on rather better – I traced him to a derelict pub in Limehouse, where he lives among a group of homeless people who have created for themselves an extraordinary 'home', making something almost admirable from what are frankly the most squalid circumstances. It transpires that this place – The East Indian Chief – was used by Holmes when he was in disguise, looking for Moriarty. Wiggins duly arrived for our meeting, but he will not talk to me of his family – he clearly harbours deep resentment. He assures me that he now manages to survive on the right side of the law, even saving a little money – in order to, as he puts it, 'better myself'. At this point in time, I did not know what he meant. He has a good brain, being entirely self-taught: he can read and write, and is attempting to build a small library – this will be one point of contact with him – indeed I gave him a small medical dictionary which he had noticed on my shelves. He was somewhat moody with me – not unlike Holmes in his secretiveness – had to be drawn out. A proud chap. Embarrassed by what he saw as his failure in the remarkable affair of the rescue. He will not be patronised, which I respect, but it does make it difficult to help him. He did not want me to talk to his companion, whom I had expected to come with him on Saturday, but didn't.

TITCH

The boy Simpson (Pat) – known as Titch. Lives in the same pub, with Wiggins. I have only been able to gather information about him from Billy. A runaway from the north of England; has an uncle in Calcutta. River people. Apparently he feels that if he had access to a small boat, he could make a living. Something ought to be possible – Wiggins himself arranged a boat for the rescue. Perhaps I can get at Wiggins through Titch, and vice versa. Strange child, rather mysterious, a little shifty even, but loyal to Wiggins, to a fault – a quality of which I wholeheartedly approve. Told Billy that Wiggins more or less saved him from the streets. Also told Billy that when Wiggins talks of 'betterment', he means that he dreams of being a doctor! If this is so – and the evidence points that way – I have him! If Holmes is right about Titch, then 'his' evasiveness and Wiggins's over protectiveness are understandable!

SHERLOCK HOLMES

Holmes believes that he has traced the relationship between Moriarty and 'white slavery'. He suspects that the evil Professor is forming a plan of hitherto unknown magnitude; that he has been using this foul trade to create a network, under the guise of which he is cooking up something truly fiendish. As Holmes has many times remarked, if only this man were to put his cunning to fruitful use, how much the world would benefit from his exceptional gifts. Wiggins, Titch, Billy, Potts and Edie could have better, richer lives. As it is, who knows where and when Moriarty will reassert his malign influence.

ANN-LI

The Changs, it would appear, are safe. Wiggins's plan to get them out of London has worked, and although the Dragons may not have been stopped altogether, their progress has been halted for the time being.

MALTRAVERS

Their agents, Maltravers and Dooley, are up before the bench in Bow Street tomorrow. I am sure they will receive a hefty sentence – Maltravers longer than Dooley, I imagine. A blow for justice!

DOOLEY

**Turn over the page to read more
Baker Street Mysteries . . .**

Read on for more Baker Street Mysteries in

The Rose of Africa

Coming Soon . . .

Billy Chizzell, the page-boy at 221b Baker Street, stood in the hall, waiting for the storm to break. His friend, Sam Wiggins, who had dropped in to see him, watched with him.

'What's going on, Billy?'

'Some nob's been to see Mr Holmes. Real posh bloke. Foreign accent.'

'Oh, him. I saw him leaving just now in a fancy carriage.'

'Looks like European royalty to me.' said Billy. 'I fancy the guv'nor will be on his way shortly, so I've taken the precaution of having a hansom-cab stand by. Where's Titch, Sam?'

'In the kitchen with Mrs. Hudson.'

'Leftovers of a nice cinnamon tart today!'

The two lads were looking up the stairs to Sherlock Holmes's study when suddenly the door burst open.

'Order me a cab, Billy!' came Holmes's cry.

Billy turned to Sam. 'What did I tell you?'

Sam grinned. 'Clever old you.'

Holmes was shouting. 'Good-bye, Watson! I must away. This mission is top secret, and my presence is required urgently!' When he had something on his mind, Holmes was like a man possessed. He swept out of his study, almost knocking Dr Watson over. He continued his imperious descent of the staircase donning his Aberdeen cape and his deerstalker hat as he went.

'Get my luggage, boy.' he shouted at Billy, who dodged past him, running *up* the stairs to collect Holmes's portmanteau. 'Out of my way, Wiggins! There will be no need for you and the team on this assignment!' Holmes ran to the door and flung it open. He would have charged straight out, but to his surprise, his way was barred by a scruffy young lad wearing a battered bowler. It was the wiry figure of Potts, who was usually game for a laugh, but on this occasion was out of breath, and looking decidedly green.

'Potts!' cried Holmes. 'What are you doing here? I have already told Wiggins The Irregulars are surplus to requirements on this case. Out of my way!'

'I need your 'elp, Mr 'Olmes,' panted Potts. 'I 'ate to ask, but you gotta 'elp me!'

'I beg your pardon, Potts. I have not a moment to spare.'

'But Mr 'Olmes, it's dead serious. Please. You gotta just 'ear me out.'

Holmes pushed past Potts, and made straight for the hansom that Billy had ordered.

'Waterloo *station*!' he called to the driver. 'With all haste!'

As Holmes was mounting the cab steps, Billy arrived, breathless, with his luggage.

Holmes grabbed it from him and called again to the driver. 'Waterloo, my man. I must catch the boat train!' The driver raised his whip, and the horse began to pull away.

Potts was jumping up and down, shouting, trying to get Holmes's attention. From the doorway, Wiggins, who had been joined by Billy and Dr Watson, watched in astonishment as Potts leapt on to the step of the moving hansom, preventing Holmes from closing the cab door. They saw Potts pleading and Holmes gesticulating, as the hansom gathered speed.

Billy turned to Sam. 'What's going on?'

'I dunno,' he replied.

They all watched as the hansom-cab sped down Baker Street.

'What the hell happened while I was getting the bag, Sam?' asked Billy.

'Potts turned up. He was in a real state. Said he wanted Mr Holmes's help.'

'He'll be lucky!' Billy remarked.

The hansom was moving so fast now that as it swung round the corner into the Marylebone Road, it looked as though Potts would be flung to the ground. However, as it disappeared out of sight, they saw Holmes reach out, draw Potts inside and slam the door.

'He *was* lucky,' said Sam dryly.

'Well, I never!' puffed Watson.

'I wonder what he wanted?' said Billy.

The three of them looked at each other.

'Yes,' said Sam. 'I wonder.'

Although he was angry with Potts, Holmes was equally curious. 'Damn you, Potts. What is it you want?'

Potts was unable to speak. 'Get your breath back and tell me. We do not have that long. Faster, driver, faster!' Holmes called out of the cab window.

Potts felt he had been sucked into a whirlpool, but launched into his tale.

'Well Mr H it's like this. 'Ave you 'eard of the Rose of Africa?'

'Indeed I have, Potts. One of the largest, most beautiful pink diamonds in the world – the most valuable stone ever to come out of the Kimberley mines of South Africa. It is pear-shaped, weighs 125.02 carats – enormous – and it is fabled to emit a pink glow.'

''Cor blimey, you know everyfing! Well, sir, it's been nicked.'

'That is hardly a surprise, Potts. It is of inestimable value, and it has a disturbed history. What is harder to comprehend is why *you* should be telling me, and why its loss should so upset you. At least it might explain why you have been to Pentonville prison.'

Potts was stunned. ''Ow do you know I've been to Pentonville?'

'The mud on the instep of your left boot is peculiar to that part of London. Tell me quickly why you are so distraught.'

The hansom-cab rattled round the corner into Gower Street, swaying violently. Clinging on for dear life, Potts continued with his tale.

'Well, sir, it's like this. The Rose was placed in one of the safety deposit boxes at the African Diamond Company in Mayfair. It's vanished. Gone. I know about it cos my Uncle 'Ector works there. Leastways 'e *did*. But they've been and gone and arrested *'im* for nickin' it. Well anyone 'oo knows my Uncle 'Ector knows that 'e couldn't 'ave done it. 'E's not the type. Steady as you like my uncle – this was 'is bowler by the way, wot 'e give me.' Potts was very fond of his Uncle Hector's old bowler hat, and as he spoke of it, he took it off and stroked it lovingly.

'Get on with it, Potts.'

'Sorry, sir. Well, 'Ector don't drink. 'E practically lives down Temperance Hall – always singing hymns and bashin' away at 'is bloomin' tambourine 'e is. Drives us nuts. 'E simply would not do a fing like this.'

'I believe you, Potts, but this constitutes no defence at all. You need evidence.'

'It gets worse, tho', Mr H.'

'Do tell me – and quickly – we are approaching Covent Garden.' Holmes was leaning forward with his chin in his hands. His eyes were intent on Potts, and his mind concentrated on the young boy's story.

'It's like this, sir. The Shift Manager, Thomas Topper by name – 'oo was a friend of 'Ector's – is found dead in the vaults.'

'Of the African Diamond Company?'

'Of the ADC, exactly so. And – 'ere comes the dodgy bit – they find 'Ector standin' over the body.'

'Oh dear, Potts.'

'It gets worse. In 'is pocket they find this bloomin' ticket. It's for a one-way steamboat trip to South Africa. Don't look good, do it?'

'It looks very bleak indeed, Potts.'

'It gets worse. On the dead body was the very gun wot Thomas Topper 'ad been shot wiv. When Inspector Lestrade arrives at the murder scene, 'e asks 'Ector 'oo done it. And 'Ector says "Me!" it's dopey. No one believes 'im.'

'Where was the diamond?'

'Gone. Not there.'

Holmes drew breath. Then he asked, 'Can you by any chance describe the murder weapon to me?'

'I can actually, sir. When we were up at Pentonville to see 'Ector, Inspector Lestrade told us it was quite small. More of a pistole like. Wiv a pearl 'andle.'

'Ah. I see.' Holmes sat back in his seat and breathed a sigh of relief. 'Potts, your uncle is quite clearly innocent.'

'Wot about the steamer ticket?'

'Irrelevant.'

'Wot about the gun?'

'Circumstantial piffle. I am confident, Potts, that your uncle will be quite safe. Unless, of course, that fool Lestrade believes him. Ah, Waterloo Bridge. We shall soon be there.'

'Wot about him admitting it, Mr H?'

'A cover.'

'Wot can I do to 'elp 'im tho', Mr H? I can't let 'Ector go to the gallows for sumfin' 'e never done. 'E's a lovely man. Wot can I do?'

'What you can do, my dear Potts, is find out *why* your uncle is lying. I suspect that fear of the gallows will play on his mind, and may well loosen his tongue.'

'You don't know 'Ector. When 'e's set on sumfin' a team of 'orses can't shift 'im. And 'e's loyal to a fault.'

'If you say so, my dear Potts, but you will find that nothing focuses the mind quite like the fear of death. Here we are. Waterloo. Forgive me I must leave you.' So saying Holmes took up his protmanteau. Without another word to Potts, he opened the cab door, and leapt out, throwing the cab driver a handful of coins as he did so. Potts watched him bound across the pavement and up the steps into Waterloo Station. As Holmes disappeared among the press of people, Potts sat contemplating Holmes's advice.

'Goodbye, Mr 'Olmes,' he said to himself. 'And fanks for nuffin'!'